# Cutters Don't Cry

*The First Book in the SoCal Series*

CREATIVE MEDIA, INC.
PO Box 6270
Whittier, California 90609-6270
United States of America

WWW.CREATIVEMEDIA.NET

Cover and Book design by Joseph Dzidrums
Cover Photo © 2010 Joseph Dzidrums. Used with permission.
Copy Editor: Elizabeth Allison

First Printing: April 2010

Library of Congress Control Number: 2010901340

ISBN 978-0-9826435-1-8          10 9 8 7 6 5 4 3 2 1

# Cutters Don't Cry

*The First Book in the SoCal Series*

A Novel by
**Christine Dzidrums**

To Joey,

My best audience, my best friend and the best thing
that ever happened to me.


With much love to: Dad, Mom, Lise, Anthony, Leah, Jeff
Joshua and Timothy.

# *Triumph*

I almost cried today. My mind whirled. My bottom lip quivered. My eyes stung.

That's a huge deal.

For the past six years, I have floated through life free from cumbersome emotions.

No boy has ever broken my heart because I have never offered it to anyone.

No girl has ever ended our friendship because I have no friends.

I run from attachment at all costs. I avoid rejection even more.

During high school my classmates fended off ulcers waiting for their SAT scores. I skipped the test-taking scene and applied to community college where no one ever gets turned down.

In my eighteen-month career at Long Beach City College, I have averaged two classes a semester. At my rate, I'll become a 34-year-old college graduate. That is, I'll graduate if I ever choose a major.

I didn't intend to become an underachieving loner. Six years ago my current state would have horrified me, but I've changed. My former self suffered from complicated, messy feelings.

At the age of 19, I cruise through life on autopilot. Every morning I drive my beat-up Chevy to school. Step on the brake for the red light. Press the gas pedal for a green light. I don't get angry if a driver cuts me off, and I never impatiently tailgate anyone. I don't speed through yellow lights because I'm never in a hurry to get anywhere.

At first college seemed even easier than high school. You're on your own in college. Professors rarely bother to learn your name. You ditch class? Teachers don't care. You skip test day? Enjoy your F. I found a warm anonymity in higher education. That's why I acquired a false sense of security that led to my stupid mistake. I got sloppy; I got caught.

Before I knew it, a school therapist named Hunter entered my life. Except, I resisted counseling. I still fight it. I usually show up to my weekly appointments and sit stoically on his couch, tossing out brief answers. "No," "Maybe," and "Not really" are my favorite selections.

On our first session together, as Hunter discussed therapy's benefits, I counted the leaves on a tree perched outside his office's cracked window.

The next week Hunter moved us to a windowless room, so I silently recited the U.S. states for 45 minutes.

Hunter didn't speak during today's visit. He just sat in his squeaky vinyl chair and smiled patiently at me all session. So, I counted items in his office: cobwebs (4), picture frames (8), carpet stains (14) and books (111).

I bolted for the door as soon as 1:50 arrived. That's when Hunter finally broke his silence.

"Charity, wait," he called.

I watched him pull a red leather book from his desk's top drawer.

"I bought you a journal," he said matter-of-factly. "I'm hoping that you'll find it easier to express your feelings through writing."

"Of course," he continued, "I'd still like to see you on a weekly basis."

A person with good manners would have thanked him. Instead, I just nodded and accepted his gift.

He added warmly, "See you next week."

Then I did something really stupid. I looked into Hunter's eyes. That's when I saw it - an expression that hovered between caring and concern.

A mixture of embarrassment and longing hit me. Pain that I've stifled for so many years engulfed me.

I opened my mouth to mutter a quick goodbye. No sound came out. So, I just darted out of his office.

A loud buzz cluttered the halls as students walked lazily to their next class. Piercing laughter, carefree squeals and loose conversation threatened my vacuous existence.

Internally, I struggled to block out what had just happened. Failure. A rush of feelings taunted me.

I busied my mind with silly distractions.

I counted silently to 20.

Hunter's compassionate eyes haunted me.

I whispered the alphabet song.

My foundation quaked.

No. Absolutely not. I could not allow this to happen. I would not return to a world of uncertainty. I needed to nip the onslaught of emotions that threatened me.

I bolted up the nearest flight of stairs. When I arrived at the second floor women's restroom, I locked myself in my usual stall. My hands trembled as I pulled a razor from my purse. I pulled up my left sleeve and pierced my skin three times. Blood escaped from my veins.

I gasped in anguish. My emotional struggle instantly took a backseat to the intense physical pain that jolted through me. My body trembled. I shut my eyes and bit my bottom lip. I rocked back and forth as I moaned softly.

After a few agonizing moments, the pain subsided. More importantly, the emotional upswell disappeared.

I waited for my heart rate to decrease before I opened my eyes. Blood populated my arm. I grabbed a wad of toilet paper and wiped my wounds.

Triumph. I had defeated my emotions - again.

As I reached into my purse for my stock of bandages, confusion seeped into my consciousness.

What just happened?

On the drive home, at each stoplight, I reached over to my arm, lifted my sleeve and touched the bandages.

I hadn't felt emotions in so long.

After I stepped into the shower, I peeled off the adhesive strips and traced each scar.

My cuts protected me from the outside world. Could one kind gesture really destroy my shelter?

Moments ago I slid into bed with this diary in hand. My pen eagerly embraced the page. As I recounted the day's events, I realized that I wanted you on this journey.

If I use this journal honestly, I can write all the things I could never admit out loud.

How I envy people who don't suffocate their emotions.

How I want to laugh again and truly feel it.

How I miss even negative feelings, like anger, disappointment and frustration.

How I yearn to put down my razor forever.

Could I really have such things, though? It's seems impossible. For much of my life, I have trained myself to believe that:

Cutters can't dream.

Cutters don't feel.

Cutters can't laugh.

And, most of all, cutters don't cry.

# Reflections on a Saturday Afternoon

Why do I cut? It's a valid question. Unfortunately, I can't offer you a concise answer.

Most people balk at the prospect of cutting into their own body. The concept seems absurd. Humans spend their lives striving to preserve their bodies. Why would someone willingly destroy his or her body?

Except, I don't view my cutting as a destructive force. The physical act keeps me safe from emotional pain that feels more threatening to me than anything a razor could inflict.

Yes, I suppose cutting poses a serious physical risk. At times I have wondered what would happen if I accidentally cut too deep one day. I've found that over the years, as my cutting continues, my tolerance for pain increases. There are times when this fear causes me to reassess my decision to cut, but I always return to my razor.

Cutting is also my own little secret. No one but Hunter (and now you) knows that I engage in self-harm. I've managed to keep my act hidden for around six years now. That's a pretty impressive feat for someone who lives in a beach city in sunny Southern California. Most people around here wear tank tops and shorts, while I walk around in long-sleeve shirts and jeans that hide my ugly scars. Sure, I get weird looks sometimes or questions like, "Aren't you hot?"

I just let people think I'm a bit strange. Better to be labeled a weirdo than to give up my self-harm. Cutting comforts me. It's an integral part of my life. I'm not sure I could survive without it.

# Quiet, Conscientious and Hardworking

Mom never married you. She never did a lot of things.

Ever since Mom was a young girl, she dreamed of opening her own travel agency. That's strange, since she has never ventured outside California's warm borders.

Shortly after Mom turned six years old, her mother died of leukemia at the age of 30. Sometimes I think it's a blessing to die young. Then you don't have to live with so many of your screw-ups. People only remember your strong traits while they lament the great potential you were unable to fulfill.

When I was 12 years old, I asked Mom how it felt to attend her mother's funeral.

"You'll find out someday," she answered.

I hated her response. It terrified me. Instead, I wish she would have wrapped her arms around me and promised never to die.

Mom didn't have a close relationship with her father. She described him as a soft-spoken man who worked hard and liked watching television. Crime dramas and sports were his favorites. He also loved a good riddle.

Mom said that her dad came home from his construction job so tired that she never bothered him. He ate his dinner in front of the TV, and Mom ate in the kitchen with her older sister Betty.

Many years ago I asked Mom if she ever missed having a mother.

"It's hard to miss something you never really had," she answered.

Aunt Betty once showed me her old family album. It only took me ten seconds to spot Mom in her second grade class photo. She was the serious looking girl in the middle row. Mom wore a crisp white shirt and a freshly pressed skirt. She stood with perfect posture, staring solemnly into the camera as if her life depended upon taking a flawless photograph. She wore the same expression in every picture in that album.

Aunt Betty even showed me Mom's old report cards once. The teachers' comments always described her as quiet, conscientious and hardworking. She never earned any grade lower than a B+, except for one year when she earned straight C's. Aunt Betty dubbed Mom's sophomore year as "The Jayson Year."

Jayson Foster spent most of his senior year in auto shop. Aunt Betty claims Jayson wasn't particularly good looking, but he could charm anyone, even Mom. He worked the front desk at Nathan's Bowling Alley after school. Sometimes Mom wandered into Nathan's hoping to get a good peek at him. She would order a soda while she pretended to watch the bowlers, but she really checked-out Jayson.

One afternoon Jayson struck up a conversation with Mom and asked her to a movie. They dated for several months. Aunt Betty had never seen Mom happier.

Jayson wasn't the world's greatest boyfriend, though. He often cancelled dates with Mom if an extra shift popped up at work. Mom pretended not to care, but Aunt Betty knew better. After he graduated from high school, Jayson phoned Mom less and less, until he stopped calling altogether. A few months later he moved to Boise, Idaho, opened an auto shop and married a local girl. Aunt Betty said Mom never got over Jayson.

I once asked Mom about Jayson. She acted like she barely remembered him. That's when I first realized that even moms lie.

# Mom: Part 2

After Jayson smashed her heart, Mom returned to her life of quiet studies and dateless Friday nights. She became determined to earn a college scholarship.

Long Beach State rewarded Mom's solid efforts with a partial scholarship. After her high school graduation, Mom moved into a two-bedroom apartment with two other college students. She landed a job at a nearby pizza parlor to finance her remaining tuition.

One day during Mom's sophomore year, she knelt on the floor wiping up spilled beer after a rowdy college crowd had invaded the joint. Suddenly, the restaurant manager summoned her to the phone. A tearful Aunt Betty informed Mom that their father had dropped dead at work after he suffered a heart attack. Aunt Betty said Mom grieved "in her own way." She scheduled her father's funeral between a history and chemistry final.

Mom isn't heartless. Her heart just never overrules her head. She's too practical to fall victim to her emotions.

After Mom buried her father, she quickly resumed her studies. She strove to graduate with a business degree in three short years. And she did just that, despite you and I nearly ruining everything for her.

# *You*

I can summarize your childhood in one paragraph. You grew up in a nuclear family in Henderson, Nevada, with two devoted parents and an older sister named Mary. When you were seven years old, your mother served dinner and then excused herself so she could sleep off a terrible headache. She never woke up. Your mom died of a brain aneurysm at the age of 32. You found her body.

That's all I know about your life until Mom entered it. On the night you graduated high school, you scored $425.00 in cash from aunts, uncles and grandparents. Your father gave you a Ford Mustang that he had spent months restoring in a friend's garage.

You initially planned to take your new car out for a quick spin, but the further you got from home, the happier you became. Eventually, you wound up on Interstate 15. You crossed the California state line 45 minutes later.

Nearly four hours later you stood on the doorstep of your good buddy Ron Ball. When he had graduated high school one year earlier than you, he moved to California to attend Long Beach State. His first day on campus he stood by the job notice board looking for employment opportunities when he noticed a cute brunette named Sutton. She smiled shyly at him when he asked her for the time. They were soon inseparable.

Sutton shared a nearby apartment with Mom and a girl named Kerri. Ron spent most of his first semester at their place. Six months later he became their full-fledged roommate. From time to time he dropped you a postcard describing California's lure. The ocean breeze and its picturesque beauty sounded so inviting that you drove straight to Ron's place on your high school graduation night.

When you arrived in Long Beach, Mom answered the door. Sutton and Ron had fled to San Diego for a weekend of surfing and drinking. Luckily, Mom took pity on you and invited you inside for a cup of coffee.

You two talked until sunrise. I don't like to think about what happened next. Let's just say that I entered the world nine months later.

# Unknown Song

I hit the alarm's snooze button four times before I finally admitted to myself that I wasn't going to school today.

After I drifted back to sleep, I had the most vivid dream. I stood on my old high school's tennis court wearing a faded T-shirt, jeans and a sapphire scarf around my neck. I clutched a package with shiny red wrapping. When I lifted the lid of the box, a beautiful gold accordion flew out of the package and into my hands.

Suddenly, a group of my old teachers shuffled out on the court in a single file line. They sat in folding chairs in front of the net and looked expectantly at me. I had never held an accordion in my life, but they waited for me to play for them.

I smiled awkwardly and then began playing the instrument with incredible passion. My song consumed me. I gripped the accordion with all my might, as I felt the highs and lows of each note with extreme sensitivity. Before I knew it, tears streamed down my face. My emotions didn't interrupt my song, though.

One by one each teacher nodded off until soon they were all sleeping during my impromptu concert. I kept playing, though. I played and played and played furiously until the barking of my neighbor's dog stirred me from my sleep.

# Eternity

Mom walked into my bedroom after dinner. She sat on my bed and folded her hands in her lap. I slouched at my desk in front of my computer. I should have been researching my Art Appreciation term paper. Instead, I had become absorbed in a solitaire game.

"How's school?" Mom asked, as she settled on my bed.

"Great," I answered, as I minimized my game.

An awkward pause followed. Mom surveyed my room.

"There's wallpaper peeling in that corner," she said. "I can fix that."

"OK," I replied.

"It won't take me long," Mom said, standing up. "I have some paste in the pantry."

"Maybe later," I answered. "I'm busy right now."

She sat down. More strained silence followed.

"What are you doing?" she finally asked.

"Homework," I answered. "I'm writing a paper for art class."

Mom looked pleased.

"I'm happy to see that you're taking your studies so seriously," she said.

I didn't answer.

After what seemed like an eternity, Mom rose from my bed.

"I'll let you get back to your homework," she said.

Mom left my room before I could respond.

# *You and Mom*

Following your initial meeting Mom spent the weekend as your personal Southern California tour guide. You visited the popular beaches, explored the Griffith Observatory and caught a game at Dodger Stadium.

Ron and Sutton returned home on Sunday evening. The four of you spent the evening drinking and chatting. When Ron encouraged you to stick around for the summer, you eagerly accepted the invitation. A few weeks later Mom got a fat positive on a pregnancy test, and you chose to remain in California permanently.

I loved that you moved to a new state on the spur of the moment. I laughed when Aunt Betty told me that you didn't even return home to fetch your clothes or any personal belongings. You just quickly acclimated to a new life.

Mom, on the other hand, dismissed your actions as "a typical thing your dad would do." She didn't find it funny like me.

Six months later you drove back to Nevada to attend your dad's funeral after he died of lung cancer. You left the service five minutes before you were scheduled to deliver the eulogy.

Mom said you smoke, too, just like your father. I once stole a cigarette from Aunt Betty's purse and lit up behind our apartment complex. When I went back inside, Mom smelled cigarette on me right away. I denied smoking, but she just gave me a hard look like she didn't believe me. I never smoked again after that.

# My Arrival

As Mom entered her second trimester, you both moved into a two-bedroom apartment in a Spanish-style building several blocks from the beach. You found a job at a nearby photography studio, while Mom continued working toward her business degree.

Once I asked Aunt Betty if you and Mom were hopelessly in love during this time. I pictured you two as romantic kids surviving in a scary world as you eagerly awaited my birth.

Aunt Betty looked at me blankly.

"They did what they had to do," she shrugged.

One scorching weekday morning in March, Mom sat by an open window at the dining room table, which had become her makeshift study area, when she felt her first contraction. I had announced my arrival.

You were sprawled on the couch watching a game show when Mom calmly announced, "It's time."

You were such a nervous wreck. Mom spent most of the drive to the hospital reassuring you.

When you pulled into the hospital parking lot, you pointed to a sign on a nearby light pole and said, "Look, they're offering CPR lessons tomorrow. We should go."

Your strange comment propelled Mom into a fit of giggles. The two of you were still grinning when you arrived in the ER.

After the hospital admitted Mom, you scoured the halls for a pay phone so you could call Aunt Betty. By the time you returned to the maternity ward, I had already arrived. Mom's doctor called me the smoothest delivery ever.

Mom felt an enormous sense of peace wash over her when she held me for the first time. Motherhood fit her perfectly. She began making immediate plans for us.

Mom said tears clouded your eyes when she first placed me in your arms. Aunt Betty once told me that she had never seen a more emotional father.

Maybe that's why it's so hard to understand why you left us nine months later.

# *Tuesday is Ditch Day*

This morning I played another game of hit the snooze button before I faced reality. I was taking a four-day weekend.

I spent the first part of the morning watching a string of game show repeats from the '60s and '70s. As I munched on some corn flakes, I wondered what had happened to the contestants on the screen. Were they happy? Were they still alive? If they were still living, were they watching the rerun of their episode, too? It must feel weird to turn on the television one day and see yourself decades younger.

It's funny but I've never envisioned myself as living a long life. Even when I was a young girl, I didn't contemplate any plans for my future. I've never imagined myself as a real adult with grown-up responsibilities. I have never thought of myself as growing old someday. Other people will marry, create children, experience life's ups and downs and slowly inch their way toward death - but not me. It'll be surprising if I make it to age 40. I'm not trying to sound morbid. It's just a belief I've long held.

When I tired of quiz shows, I snuggled back into bed for a nap. I've always been able to sleep anytime I want. It doesn't matter where I am, I can fall asleep instantly. Mom has the opposite problem. She has difficulty getting a good night's rest unless there's complete silence.

Lately, I've slept more than usual, though. I now go to bed about two hours earlier than normal. In fact, most of the day I wait for nighttime so I can escape for hours. Imagine the peace I'd possess if I could sleep all the time.

## *"Everywhere"*

Ten weeks after my birth, Mom earned a B.S. degree in Business from Long Beach State. Four weeks later she landed a modest sales job at a local insurance company. She quickly settled into her brown leather chair in a corner cubicle and has remained there for nearly 19 years. Mom's boss promoted her to a managerial position many years ago, but she kept her cubicle. She claimed it was "too much of a nuisance" to move her belongings to her new office across the hall.

Mom loved that her job's location offered her a short commute to work. You could even walk to your job at the photo studio. Sometimes on your way to work, you dropped me off at a nearby nursery, but most of the time, Aunt Betty, who often worked from home as a court reporter, cared for me.

Apparently, you tried to settle into your unchartered role as a responsible adult, but you felt overwhelmed. You hated your job's artistic restrictions. You especially despised weekends when you worked the wedding circuit.

"People are boring," you complained. "Where's the beauty in staged poses?"

Shortly after I turned eight months old, your boss fired you for excessive absences. Aunt Betty said you seemed more relieved than upset.

Mom encouraged you to take some college courses. You grudgingly signed up for business classes at Long Beach City College. Mom paid almost two hundred dollars for your textbooks, but you only lasted three weeks.

With no job and no school claiming your time, you became my primary caretaker. Aunt Betty said you were crazy about me but too irresponsible. Sometimes you loaded me into a stroller and walked the neighborhood aimlessly just to get out of our cramped apartment.

One weekday morning you and Ron packed me in your car and drove down to San Diego to visit some friends. An afternoon of surfing and drinking spilled into the evening, and we wound up spending the night there. Your "erratic behavior" infuriated Mom.

About two weeks later Mom came home one evening to find the door unlocked and you and I missing. Worried, she scoured the neighborhood. Aunt Betty came over to organize a search. Finally, half an hour later, you casually walked back into the apartment with me in my stroller.

When Mom demanded to know where we'd been for nearly five hours, you offered a flippant, "Everywhere."

A few days later Mom returned home to discover us missing again. She finally hunted us down at the beach. You sat cross-legged on the sand staring at the ocean with me on your lap. She hissed at you all the way home, but you barely blinked an eye. You didn't even apologize for worrying her.

Eventually, you stopped leaving the apartment altogether. You just parked yourself on the couch all day and watched TV with a glazed expression. You only stirred to change my diaper or feed me.

Finally, Mom had enough of your flakiness. She came home one night to find that you hadn't made dinner – again. Mom said if you were so unhappy with your life, you should leave. Then she stormed off to the kitchen to boil some pasta.

When she returned to the living room a few minutes later, I sat crying in my playpen and you were gone. We never saw you again. You didn't even take any of your clothes – only your camera. Aunt Betty said that your leaving was the most responsible thing you had ever done.

# *$20.00*

I did hear from you again, twice. You sent me a birthday card on my sixth birthday. It said you thought of me often, and you would visit soon.

Your next contact occurred on my eighth birthday. This time you tucked a $20.00 bill into my card. That money meant the world to me. I kept the cash in my top dresser drawer for years. I thought you'd show up one day, and we would spend that 20 bucks together.

Mom always grew quiet when I talked about wanting to meet you. Aunt Betty once implied that I shouldn't ask about you because it hurt Mom greatly to hear your name. Ashamed, I finally stopped mentioning you. I never stopped thinking about you, though.

Why won't Mom talk about you? She shared nearly two years of her life with you, but she acts like you never existed.

Do you ever talk about us? Are you now sharing your life with someone else? Do you have a new family now? If so, do they know about us? Have you thought of Mom even once? Do you think about me when you see other girls my age? Have you ever imagined what I look like now? Do you wonder if Mom ever married someone? If you found out that she had, would you be jealous?

I think it's unfair that you have nine months of memories with me, but I have none of you. Where are my memories?

Do you want to know how I eventually spent that $20.00 bill? I walked to Patti's Pet Shop and bought a red eared slider turtle. I named her Judy. Three days after I brought Judy home, I woke up one morning to find her sprawled on her back - dead.

# The Sunday Paper

I awoke at 6 a.m. this morning. Go figure. After a long, warm shower, I sat at the kitchen table reading the *Press-Telegram* over a glass of orange juice and a slice of raisin toast.

As usual I flipped to the classified ads section – the personal ads to be exact. One entry caught my eye:

*MSF - Met you Friday at Jill's Bakery at 9 AM. You're Russian. I'm Spanish. We connected. I was scared to ask for your number. Same time this Friday?*

I keep thinking about this Spanish man attempting to reconnect with some Russian woman he met at a coffee shop. It baffles me that two total strangers could "connect" so easily. How can people feel so secure that they can instantly strike up a conversation with someone they don't even know?

I can't carry a conversation with my own mother without feeling awkward. How could I ever have a breezy chat with a stranger? I would spend the whole time worrying about every word I said and each facial expression I made. Even when someone at the mall asks me for the time, or a classmate asks me for an extra pencil, I cringe inwardly. I'm sure that in the small exchange we had, they came away thinking I'm some weirdo who is incapable of having a normal conversation.

It's not like I ever have to worry about some guy approaching me at a coffee shop, or any other place, though. No one ever sees me. That's not me feeling sorry for myself. It's the truth.

I will never be the type of girl who garners attention from a guy - or anyone else for that matter. People rarely see me, and I'm perfectly content with that, too. I don't need to be noticed. I don't want someone invading my personal world. I'm alone and that's the way I like it.

## Uneventful Tuesday

School was uneventful today. I should have ditched.

My Cultural Anthropology teacher cancelled our class, so I had a two-hour break while I waited for Art Appreciation at 1 p.m. I walked to the student center, bought a diet soda and planted myself in front of a big TV. A group of students voted to watch back-to-back soap operas, so I sat watching the shows while wishing I had slept in instead.

On my walk to Art Appreciation, I passed by two girls sitting on a bench right outside the food court. One of the girls, a slight redhead, looked very skinny and withdrawn. The other girl, athletic-looking with a dirty blonde ponytail, was telling her how she'd told off a customer at the clothing store where she worked. The redhead had clearly stopped listening to her friend's story. She stared off in the distance with a dull expression. Athletic Girl didn't even notice her friend's lack of attention.

The redhead's facial features were sunken in. Visible bags underlined her eyes and highlighted her colorless skin. Her dull red hair hung limply, and her black sweater swallowed her tiny frame. She looked how I felt.

I stared at her longer than I should have, because she suddenly snapped to attention, as if she realized someone was observing her. Her eyes darted my way just as I averted my eyes.

Athletic Girl still chattered away. Her voice grew louder in anticipation of the story's big payoff.

"Look at your friend," I wanted to shout at the athletic girl. "She needs your help. Do something!"

Of course, I didn't say anything. I just hurried toward my art class.

# *Failure*

Our art professor, Ms. Verdon, didn't lecture today. She played the second part of a controversial documentary about a so-called child prodigy of abstract art. Since I had missed part one on Tuesday, I rested my head on my desk and took a 50-minute nap.

Believe it or not, I started out as a good student. In fact, I was meticulous at a young age.

My babysitter, Audra Martin, wore a back brace thanks to her scoliosis. She had mild acne and often spent hours talking on the phone to some boy named Michael.

When I was six years old, Audra sat at our kitchen table working on her homework while I played waitress.

"Do you want coffee or milk?" I asked.

"Uh, coffee," she answered.

"We only have decaf," I apologized.

I poured imaginary coffee into a plastic teacup and placed it on a cocktail napkin.

"Thank you, Charity," she smiled.

I waited for Audra to take a drink.

She held the cup to her lips and made slurping noises.

"This milk tastes delicious," she raved.

"You ordered coffee," I scowled.

Audra paused.

"That's what I said," she answered unconvincingly. "It's the best coffee ever."

"No, you didn't," I challenged. "You said milk. I heard you."

Audra weighed her options, and then her face brightened.

"Hey, Charity," she said. "I just remembered something. Would you like a present?"

"Yes," I answered.

I slid onto a chair and looked expectantly at Audra.

"Before I give it to you," she bargained, "you have to promise to behave until your mom comes home. No whining or crying."

"I promise," I answered.

Audra reached into her red nylon backpack. She presented me with a Sleeping Beauty coloring book and a pack of crayons.

"They're all yours," she sang.

I flipped through my new book.

"Thank you," I beamed.

She patted me on the shoulder.

"You're welcome," she smiled. "Now why don't you color a picture for me? Really take your time, OK? Make it look perfect."

"I will," I vowed.

I selected a picture of Sleeping Beauty climbing a stairway toward her treacherous fate, carefully filling in the princess' long hair with a yellow crayon. Next, I lightly colored her dress pink. Then my hand slipped. My crayon ventured out of bounds.

Deeply absorbed in her homework, Audra didn't notice my mistake. I frowned at my coloring job then ripped the marred page from the book.

Audra looked up confused and asked, "What are you doing?"

"I messed up," I apologized. "I'm starting over."

Audra nodded. She returned to her studies.

Next, I chose a picture of the prince and Sleeping Beauty riding on a beautiful stallion. I colored in the princess' hair and dress once more. Then I set to work on the horse. I lightly shaded his body with a brown tint and picked a black crayon for his hooves.

Audra glanced at my drawing approvingly.

"That's so beautiful, Charity," she fawned. "You're very talented."

I blushed and soaked up her approval.

"Thank you," I answered.

"I like that you made the horse brown instead of white," Audra said.

My hand, holding a black crayon, froze mid-air.

"What do you mean?" I asked.

"It's a white horse in the movie," she answered.

I stared crushed at the picture.

"You made a better choice," Audra quickly assured me. "It makes your drawing different."

She closed her book, stood up and stretched.

"I need to make a phone call," Audra said, as she walked toward the living room. "I'll be right back. Keep coloring."

After I heard her dial a number and ask for Michael, I tore the page from my book and began a new picture.

The cycle continued for the next hour. I'd start coloring a drawing, make a mistake, rip out the page and choose a new picture. By the time Audra returned, my coloring book had dwindled down to three pages.

Audra stared at the crumpled papers strewn across the floor.

"What's going on?" she asked bewildered.

I burst into tears, ran to my room and threw myself on my bed.

Audra followed closely. She tapped lightly on my open door.

"Charity?" she asked. "Can I please come in?"

I didn't answer. My small body shook with sobs. Shame washed over me. I had ruined my beautiful gift.

Audra sat beside me.

"Shh," she soothed.

"I'm sorry that I didn't make it perfect," I apologized.

"Don't cry," Audra said, as she wiped tears from my face.

I cried harder.

"It's OK, Charity," she said softly. "It's just a coloring book."

Except it wasn't all right. Was I really so hopeless that I couldn't color a simple page without making errors?

"Come on," Audra said. "Let's make a cup of hot cocoa and watch TV."

Though I didn't feel like leaving my room, I obeyed my babysitter.

"Do you like marshmallows or whipped cream in your hot chocolate?" Audra asked sweetly, as she led me to the kitchen.

I shrugged my shoulders indifferently. Audra's sweet tone felt so confusing to me. I had messed up. I hadn't colored a picture perfectly as she had told me to. My blunder ate away at me. I couldn't just swallow my disappointment with a cup of cocoa. Didn't she realize that I deserved to be punished for my failure?

# *Jill's*

Guess who actually tumbled out of bed early this morning? I walked to Jill's Bakery. Spanish Guy would be there at 9 a.m. to see if Russian Girl showed. I wanted to see what happened.

I scanned my surroundings when I arrived. An old man, around 80, sat by the front door reading the paper and eating a lemon bar. Strike one. A 30-something man in blue jeans and an Orange County Fair shirt sat across from a woman and a baby. Strike two. Finally, a blond surfer in a worn out T-shirt, Bermuda shorts and flip-flops rounded out the scene. Strike three.

I walked to the front counter and asked for a cinnamon bun. As I waited for my order, the front door opened. I spun around. A dark-haired man in his late 30s / early 40s glanced quickly around the room before he walked toward the counter. He was dressed in khakis and a white button down shirt and appeared slightly anxious. Spanish Guy!

After the cashier handed me my food, I picked a seat in the corner next to the family. I spent the next hour pretending not to watch Spanish Guy as he pretended not to watch the front door. Russian Girl never showed.

After Spanish Guy finished his scone and cup of coffee, which he ate and drank as slowly as possible, he stood up with a resigned expression and walked quickly out the door. If I had the capacity to feel, my heart would have broken for him.

# Friday Afternoon

I'm writing during a school break. In Oceanography today Professor Mitchell lectured about the Coriolis effect. I enjoy the class more when we have field trips to beaches or aquariums, but those days are rare.

In thirty minutes I have my first session with Hunter since the day he gave me this journal. What if he asks if I've written in it? He might want details if I say yes.

Last night I couldn't sleep. This nagging feeling plagued me. I wanted to tell Hunter about you. I even wanted to talk to him about the cutting, the numbness, and the hopelessness. Part of me really yearns to spill my guts out to him.

I don't want to be like Spanish Guy. I can't let an opportunity to say something pass me by, or I might not get another chance.

Every so often I recall flashes of my former life. There were times I laughed so hard, I gasped for air. Some nights I went to bed with flutters of excitement because the next day would bring Christmas or my birthday or a vacation. Smiles sometimes happened - just because.

Perhaps Hunter can help me recapture those emotions. Not every feeling stung. Some felt downright wonderful. Maybe it's worth weeding through the bad to experience the good.

I think I'll finally open up to Hunter today. He'll be so surprised when I unleash all my pent up thoughts, but I truly trust him. If we work together then we might find some hope for me yet.

# Silence

I lost my nerve.

What happened when I stepped into Hunter's office? Nothing. I clammed up.

"How's it going, Charity?" he asked.

"Fine," I answered.

*Say something. Thank him for the journal. Tell him that you're writing in it nearly everyday.*

He always began our session with the same question.

"Would you like to discuss anything in particular today?" he asked.

"Nope," I said.

*Speak!*

"Have you had an opportunity to write in your journal yet?" he asked easily.

*Here's your chance.*

"Not yet," I answered quickly.

*What are you doing?*

"Try writing down your thoughts," Hunter encouraged. "I have a few patients who were initially skeptical about keeping a journal. They tried it out, though, and they really grew to love the process."

I nodded.

"You'd be surprised what you can learn about yourself through writing," he smiled.

I nodded again.

Dead air mocked me.

*Help me. Teach me how to feel again.*

Hunter sat patiently waiting for me to say something - anything.

"How are your classes going?" Hunter finally asked.

"Good," I answered.

*Guide me toward a normal life. I want to wake up with a purpose. Life's not worth living if I continue on this pointless journey.*

"Do you have any special plans for this weekend?" Hunter asked.

"Nope," I replied.

*I'm trapped in a state of vacuity. Why would I have any plans?*

Hunter cleared his throat and adjusted his tie.

*I'm sorry for wasting your time. I apologize for making you sit here for nearly an hour every week while I chicken out of telling you how I really feel.*

50 minutes later I gathered my belongings from the floor.

"See you next week," Hunter said.

"See you next week," I echoed.

# Daniel, My 'Stepfather'

Right after you bailed on us, Mom took a second job. She found work in the cash office at Rivera's Department Store. For seven years she worked there three nights a week and all day Saturdays. After some shifts she would grab a bite to eat with her manager named Daniel.

Aunt Betty or Audra sometimes dropped me off at Rivera's ten minutes before it closed. I'd sit transfixed in front of a giant row of TV sets until Mom completed her work. I felt so special when workers ushered the customers out the door, but they allowed me to stay after hours.

I remember on one occasion, I couldn't tear my eyes away from a children's fantasy movie that played on a big screen.

"Your daughter is a regular couch potato," Daniel joked to my mom.

"Yes," Mom said disapprovingly. "She gets that glazed expression whenever she's caught up in a movie or TV show - just like her father."

"Well, there are worse things that could happen," Daniel said good-naturedly.

Mom's comparison bothered me. I felt like I'd done something wrong - as if I had let her down.

She also had the same disdain in her voice a few months earlier when I became enraged with Aunt Betty for telling Mom that I had a crush on Stephen Sparks, the stud of my first grade class.

"You didn't get that temper from me," Mom said with a roll of her eyes.

At that moment in Rivera's Department Store, I vowed to never give Mom another reason to compare me to you. I knew that any comparisons made would not be favorable ones.

I also didn't want to give Daniel any reason to dislike me. He could do no wrong in my eyes. I worshipped him.

Daniel always made time to chat with me, even on Sale Saturdays. He liked Mom a lot, but he genuinely cared about me, too. He always seemed interested in hearing my stories about school or home life. I always waited for the moment when he'd hand me a quarter, and I'd race to the vintage gum ball machine by the front door. I once looked so disappointed after a white gum ball came down the chute that Daniel ran to register five and had the cashier make change for a dollar. He then handed me four quarters.

"Now you have four times the chance of getting a good color," he winked.

On my next try I scored a purple gum ball. Daniel let me keep the other three quarters. I later dropped them in my plastic piggy bank at home.

I always fantasized that Daniel would marry Mom, and she would become a stay-at-home mother. I even sometimes wished she'd get fired from her jobs so we'd spend more time together. I always felt guilty about that daydream.

Sometimes I imagined Daniel as my father. I'd pretend that I had disobeyed him in some way. When he would punish me, I'd feign indignation, but I secretly enjoyed it.

Over time I ached for my fantasies to come true, but I only felt empty when they didn't. Letdowns take too much out of you. So, I eventually stopped dreaming altogether.

# Saturday Afternoon

Mom wants to reupholster our couch. She and Aunt Betty planned an outing to the Garment District this afternoon to buy fabric.

I stood at the counter preparing a peanut butter and jelly sandwich when they walked in the kitchen. As usual, I tensed up when Aunt Betty entered the room.

"I have a measuring tape in here somewhere," Mom said, as she rummaged through our junk drawer.

"Hi, Sweetie," Aunt Betty smiled.

"Hi," I answered, as I spread strawberry jam on my wheat bread.

"Are you coming with us today?" she asked.

I shook my head and placed a dirty knife in the dishwasher.

"How come?" Aunt Betty insisted.

"Charity never wants to do anything anymore," Mom said, as she pulled out a cloth tape measure from the drawer.

I glared at Mom. I hated when she talked about me like I wasn't in the room. Mom ignored my shooting dagger.

"Come with us, Charity," Aunt Betty urged. "We're going to grab lunch, too."

"Don't waste your breath," Mom said.

"We're going to eat at Phillipe's," Aunt Betty said. "You love their French-dipped sandwiches."

"No, thanks," I told her.

"Why not?" she demanded.

"I have homework," I said.

"Can't you do it tonight after we get back?" Aunt Betty asked.

"I can't," I said firmly. "Have a nice time, though."

I picked up my sandwich and left the room. I didn't head straight to my bedroom, though. Instead, I hovered in the hallway by the kitchen door. I sensed they were going to talk about me.

"What's her issue?" Aunt Betty asked.

"Who knows," Mom said.

"Have you asked her what's wrong?" Aunt Betty persisted.

"There's no point," Mom replied dismissively. "It's always something with her nowadays."

"She's so moody," Aunt Betty scoffed.

"Just like her father," Mom answered.

# Responsibilities

I'm not anything like you.

Even at my laziest stage, I've stayed in school. I haven't given up. I keep going even when life seems hopeless. I have never dissolved into a puddle of self-pity.

I don't break promises. I also try not to let people down.

I would never abandon my child. Even if she was a mistake… Even if I didn't want her, I would take care of her. I wouldn't make someone else bear the entire burden of my screw-up.

I wouldn't use depression as an excuse for my selfish behavior.

I wouldn't waste my nights drinking and watching television when I should be looking for a job.

I wouldn't get so absorbed in my own problems that I neglected my responsibilities.

Before I left yesterday's session with Hunter, he reminded me that I could call him if I ever need to talk.

A man who's practically a stranger offers me his ear anytime, but I can't call my own father.

# The World's Funniest Joke

A few months ago I grappled with restlessness, so I drove aimlessly around town.

Eventually, I pulled into my former elementary school's parking lot. The school bell signaled the end of the day. Children filtered out of their classrooms and ran to their waiting guardians.

A redheaded boy walked cautiously toward a maroon minivan, as he carried a big *papier-mâché* airplane. His mother jumped out of the car to help him. Her efforts only made him more nervous. He struggled to maintain his balance, but he eventually made it inside the car with his art project intact.

A chunky brunette with wire-rimmed glasses too small for her large oval face appeared next. She looked about eight. This girl burst through a chain link gate and headed toward downtown. I watched with curiosity as she swung her lunchbox and sang off-key at the top of her lungs. A few parents smiled at her. Some kids snickered. She didn't acknowledge any of them.

Suddenly, her song stopped. She cocked her head and puckered her lips in deep concentration. Then she burst into laughter like she'd just told herself the world's funniest joke. She had a great laugh, too. It originated deep from her belly.

My curiosity turned to awe. How could someone so young and imperfect looking harbor such confidence? Could she hear how awful she sang? Did she not care how crazy she looked laughing all by herself?

I want that girl's immunity to the world's scrutiny. I envy anyone who feels so comfortable in his or her skin that they can laugh out loud when no one else is around.

## *That Independence Day*

When I was seven years old, Mom and I walked to the beach for a Fourth of July picnic. I wore my red, white and blue bathing suit and brand new sandals.

As soon as my feet touched the sand, I flung off my shoes, raced toward the ocean and threw myself into the water.

"Be careful," Mom called.

I splashed in the waves for what seemed like hours. My suit's silver sequins sparkled in the sun.

Suddenly, I noticed a petite blonde girl a few feet away. She hid shyly behind her mom's slight frame. Her eyes fixed on me.

As I enjoyed my audience, I held my breath and dunked my head underwater. When I came up for air, I still felt her stare.

"Charity," Mom called, "It's time for lunch."

I waved to my mother and swam back to shore. The sun's warmth hugged my skin as Mom threw a towel around my shoulders and then tickled me. I squirmed away with laughter.

We sat on a blanket and opened our picnic basket. Mom had packed chicken salad sandwiches and fruit salad. We ate chocolate chip cookies for dessert.

Mom sipped her iced tea and shielded her eyes from the sun's rays. She looked so young and pretty.

"We'll go shopping for more summer clothes tomorrow," she said.

I nodded and popped a cookie in my mouth.

Later that day we walked along the shore and collected seashells. We chatted about school, clothes and boys.

Out of the corner of my eye, I caught that girl watching me again. It felt good.

# Monday - The Starfish

Today our oceanography class traveled to Laguna Beach's tide pools. I might major in oceanography. I could join a research team and spend my workdays outside in the warm air. I've always hated the idea of being holed up in an office job. My eyes would drill a hole in the clock waiting for my lunch hour to arrive.

There's a cute guy in my class named Pablo. Today when he squinted at the sun, the corners of his eyes turned crinkly. I wish I had the courage to talk to him.

I stood watching a sailboat in the distance. Suddenly, I noticed a bright color in a nearby tide pool. A red starfish lay a few feet away. I snapped photos of it with my digital camera.

As we headed back to the parking lot, I showed my pictures to Professor Mitchell. He told me that starfish have two stomachs. They also have an eye on each arm. We made more small talk. I felt almost normal.

"That's a beautiful picture," he said. "Can you make me a copy for class?"

"Sure," I said casually.

"Are you a photographer?" he asked.

I paused.

"No," I answered, "but I used to know someone who was."

## *Monday Night/Tuesday Morning*

I couldn't sleep last night. The hours kept ticking away until suddenly it was 5:15 a.m. I thought of writing to you, but I didn't have anything interesting to say.

Instead, I turned on my desk lamp and tried to cram in some assigned reading for Art Appreciation. I read a few paragraphs but retained nothing.

Finally, I jumped out of bed and threw on some warm clothes and a jacket. I gently opened my bedroom door. With Mom being a light sleeper, I tiptoed into the living room.

I reached the front door, unlatched the lock and slipped outside into the dark, chilly morning.

Our usually bustling neighborhood seemed eerie in its stillness. An overflow of cars crammed the street.

Cold air stung my hands, so I shoved them into my pant pockets. I walked past a closed gas station, crossed the street and continued heading south.

I'm fully aware that a young woman walking by herself in a large city in the wee hours of the morning wasn't exactly the brightest idea. You don't have a right to worry about me doing reckless things, though. If you truly cared about my well-being, you'd still be in my life.

Moments later I passed a green Craftsman house. An older woman in a flimsy robe watched from her slightly open front door as her black poodle lifted its leg on a palm tree in her front yard.

"Good job, Oliver," she mumbled sleepily.

A few blocks later I walked past a fast food restaurant just as a man, probably the manager, got out of his car. He walked sluggishly toward the restaurant's front door as he jangled keys in his right hand. I looked away when our eyes met.

Undeterred, he muttered, "Morning."

"Morning," I echoed, so quietly that he could not possibly have heard me.

Minutes later I arrived at the beach. I hovered by an empty walkway overlooking the sand before settling on a concrete bench dedicated to a young man who had lost his life at sea. The ocean sounded inviting as its waves gently washed ashore.

I stared into the darkness for over an hour, barely budging the entire time. Shadows soon formed. Dawn slowly appeared. The sky brightened a remarkable shade of orange. The sound of car engines starting filtered through the air as people began their workday. Then the sun rose grandly, splashing a vibrant red into our part of the world.

A jogger stopped abruptly just a few feet from me. He huffed and puffed as he stared at the sky with a mesmerized expression.

"Wow," he said breathlessly.

Meanwhile, I felt nothing.

# *"Pieces of You"*

I'm fairly certain you never loved Mom, and she never loved you. I can deal with that. I wonder, though, if you two even liked each other.

Whenever I would ask about you, Mom offered vague answers.

"He had a tough personality to figure out," she would always answer.

When I was a little girl, I didn't miss you. Mom and I were once so close that I never felt a void in my world. It seemed like we'd formed a special mother/daughter club. Other members were not allowed.

I didn't envy kids with two parents and many siblings. My two-bedroom apartment with just Mom for a roommate suited me fine.

Then one day in fourth grade, I needed a baby photo for a class project. I shuffled through Mom's important papers' box, when I came across a picture of you that I'd never seen.

You sat in our living room with a half-eaten sandwich in your left hand. Your mischievous brown eyes mocked the camera as you wore a crooked smirk. You looked so happy and carefree. I didn't see a troubled soul at all.

I stared at that photo forever. Suddenly, I ached for my father. I needed you.

After I made that discovery, you consumed my thoughts for a long time. I missed you terribly. I envied anyone with an active father in his or her life.

I felt guilty for wanting you, though. Mom had worked so hard to fill your absence in my life. Yet, I still wanted more. I needed you.

Sometimes I'd walk through a crowded mall and wonder if you might be there, too. You could have been just a few feet away, and I wouldn't have known.

When Mom and I would go to a movie theater, I'd listen to the laughter filling the air and wonder if your laugh mingled with everyone else's.

When we'd shop at the supermarket, I'd search shopper's faces for traces of your features: the trouble-making eyes, the lazy grin or the speck of red in your hair that I sadly didn't inherit.

Then I went through a stage where I convinced myself you had died in a tragic car accident. I even mourned you for a week before I cornered Mom one day as she sat at the kitchen table paying bills.

"Dad's dead, isn't he?" I blurted out.

"What?" she asked. "Why would you ask such a question?"

I held my breath.

"No," Mom answered firmly. "He's not dead. Do you honestly believed that I would keep something like that from you?"

"You wouldn't," I assured her. "But we haven't heard from him in thirteen years. What if he died and we never knew it?"

"Your father isn't dead, Charity," she said cautiously. "If anything bad had happened to him, we'd have heard about it by now."

"How would we know if we never hear from him?" I asked.

Mom's face softened. I suddenly regretted saying anything at all.

"Charity, we've lived in the same apartment since you were born," she said gently. "We're not hard to find."

Then it hit me - hard. Mom was right. You could find me easily. You just chose not to.

Nowadays, I don't obsess over you, but I think about you more than you probably think about me. Would I recognize you if I spotted you on the street? Would you know I'm your daughter if you saw me?

What if you've secretly followed me around all these years? Were you the guy at Portfolio Coffeehouse who asked me for the time last month? Were you the man who once tapped me on the shoulder at the grocery store to tell me I'd accidentally dropped a $5.00 bill from my purse? Maybe my "thank you" made your day.

I inherited my dark brown hair and hazel eyes from Mom. We both tilt our head when we're deep in thought. We're suckers for puppies, babies and panda bears.

We also have our differences. My hair gets frizzy after a shower; Mom's hair always stays straight. My fair skin burns with the slightest sun exposure; Mom has a great tan. I struggle with simple math; Mom can solve complex math problems in mere seconds.

Where's the rest of my identity? What did you leave me? Which pieces of you live in me?

## *Impressionism*

I sat in Art Appreciation class today waiting impatiently for Professor Verdon to pass out our tests. I had spent hours last night cramming for the Renaissance period and needed to start my exam before the information leaked out of my brain.

When Verdon reached our row, Brent What's-His-Name said, "I forgot to bring a number two pencil."

So, what did Verdon do? She walked back to her desk, test papers still in her hand, and rummaged for a pencil for the flake.

My former high school classmate, Kristin Pinkins, came to our row's rescue.

"Hey, Professor Verdon," she called. "Can the people who were responsible enough to bring their pencils have their tests now?"

I cheered silently.

Brent What's-His-Name turned calmly toward Kristin.

"Chill," he advised.

He looked at me for moral support; I looked away.

By the time I finally held my test, Brent had a number two pencil courtesy of some loud talker in the front row.

I scribbled my name on the exam and scanned the first page.

Question One: List three characteristics of an Impressionist painting.

Question Two: Which artist painted *La Moulin De La Galette*?

I checked the rest of the exam. Every question dealt with the Impressionism era.

I glanced at my classmates. Everyone seemed immersed in his or her test. No one seemed surprised by the questions.

I had misread the class syllabus and studied the wrong chapter.

I eyed my test with trepidation. How could I possibly answer the questions correctly?

Question Three: Which painting has been called a great picture of urban life in the late 19th century?

After I watched the sunrise last Tuesday, I walked back home, crawled into bed and slept until noon. If I had attended that day's exam review, I'd have realized that the test covered the Impressionism era. Heck, if I bothered going to class on any semi-regular basis, I'd have known what to expect on the exam.

I would not waste time taking a test I had no prayer of passing. So, I spent the remainder of the class doodling on the back of my exam paper. When classmates began finishing the test and filing out of the classroom, I calmly closed my untouched exam and dropped it on Verdon's desk.

Then I hurried to the upstairs bathroom and I cut.

# *Friday*

I never should have left my warm bed this morning. Today's session with Hunter went disastrously. I'm finished with therapy.

A few minutes into our session, after I had told Hunter that everything was fine, he set down his clipboard, placed his hands on his knees and looked squarely at me.

"Charity, I'm concerned that we aren't progressing as much I would like," he said.

I nodded, simply because I didn't know how else to respond.

"You do understand that you get out of therapy what you put into it, right?" he asked.

I nodded again.

"How do you think our sessions are going?" he prodded.

I shrugged.

Hunter let out a gentle sigh and ran his fingers through his sandy brown hair.

"Your apathetic attitude concerns me," he said. "Are you this indifferent in all areas of your life?"

"I guess," I answered.

Hunter smiled wryly.

"What brings you joy?" he asked suddenly.

"Pardon?" I replied in surprise.

"What things in life bring you pleasure?" he asked. "And I will not accept a shrug for an answer."

I thought about his question honestly. Seconds ticked away. I felt mortified, but I simply could not offer an answer.

"It can be anything," he coaxed. "Big or small."

I desperately searched for a response.

"Do you enjoy singing in the shower?" he asked gently. "Are there any TV shows that you schedule your day around? Do you have any pets you adore?"

Silence flooded the room as I searched the floor for answers. Blood rushed to my cheeks.

"I don't have anything that makes me happy," I finally whispered, unable to meet his eyes.

Hunter didn't respond. For a moment I thought he hadn't heard me.

"Well that's not good," he finally said compassionately. "Everyone needs some pleasure in their life."

I felt tears gather in my eyes, so I bit the inside of my mouth until I tasted blood.

"How are you sleeping?" he asked.

"Sometimes I sleep a lot. Sometimes I can't sleep at all," I admitted.

"When you sleep a lot, how many hours are you asleep?" Hunter asked.

I wanted to lie. I wanted to tell the truth.

"Sometimes I sleep about 12 hours at night and also take a few naps during the day," I said.

Hunter nodded.

"How about the nights when you can't sleep?" he asked. "How long does it take before you eventually drift off to sleep?"

This time *I* ran my fingers through my hair. I had come this far, so I might as well continue being honest.

"Five or six hours," I answered.

Hunter stared at me incredulously.

"You're sometimes awake for five or six hours before you fall asleep?" he asked.

"I'm in college," I said meekly. "I'm supposed to have a crazy schedule."

"No one should stay awake for six hours before they fall asleep," Hunter said firmly.

I played with my hands in my lap.

"Charity, does depression run in your family?" Hunter asked softly.

I'm pretty sure the color drained from my face.

"My mother never gets depressed," I told him.

Hunter flipped open my patient file and ruffled through his notes.

"If I recall correctly from an earlier conversation, you have no contact with your father," he said.

I didn't respond.

"Do you know anything about him?" Hunter asked. "Has anyone said if he ever struggled with depression?"

I stared out the window. My throat tightened.

"I ask for a reason," Hunter said. "Children may be predisposed towards depression if one, or both, of their parents suffer from it."

Resentment surfaced in me. I didn't like the feelings that Hunter attempted to uncover. He immediately sensed my mood shift.

"Does my suggestion that you might suffer from depression upset you?" Hunter asked.

"Yes," I answered.

"Why?" he asked casually.

"Because I'm not like him," I said icily. My tone surprised me.

"So, your father did deal with depression?" Hunter persisted.

"I've heard him described as very troubled," I answered sarcastically. "I think he was a weak man who couldn't get his act together."

"Or perhaps, like many people who battle mental illness, he suffered greatly," Hunter countered quietly.

"He suffered?" I asked in disbelief. "I'm the one who grew up without a father because that deadbeat didn't stick around to help my mom raise me."

My comment rang throughout the room.

"Go on," Hunter urged.

"No," I snapped. "You're not going to get me to talk about that loser."

Hunter gazed thoughtfully at me for nearly a minute.

"Charity, I have an idea," he finally said. "I'd like to refer you to a psychiatrist I know. He works in Lakewood. Are you familiar with that area?"

My mouth dropped open.

"He's a great doctor," he told me. "I wouldn't recommend him if I didn't have complete faith in his abilities."

"Your erratic sleeping habits, your disinterest in things, lack of enjoyment in life—all these things are often signs of depression," Hunter continued. "That's why I'd like Doctor Peters to evaluate you. Of course, we should continue our weekly sessions."

"Why can't you evaluate me?" I asked.

"I'm not a doctor," he replied. "I'm a therapist."

"And what if this doctor says I am depressed?" I asked. "What then?"

"We will find the best methods of treating it, so it stops disrupting your life," Hunter said calmly.

"With medication?" I asked suspiciously.

"Sometimes," Hunter replied. "Let's not jump the gun, though. Let Doctor Peters evaluate you first."

I stood up.

"Where are you going?" Hunter asked.

"I'm not putting drugs in my body," I snapped.

"No one can make you do anything without your permission," Hunter tried to assure me. "Now please sit down, so we can continue discussing this matter."

"I think we're done here," I hissed, as I headed for the door.

"Charity," he called.

I slammed the door and didn't look back. Just like someone else I know.

# *Saturday Showdown*

Aunt Betty came over today to teach Mom the fine art of tamale making.

As I stood by the trash can peeling an orange, Aunt Betty eyed my ratty sweatshirt.

"Why are you wearing long sleeves when it's so stuffy in here?" she asked.

I considered rolling up my sleeves and showing her my scars just to shut her up, but I didn't.

Aunt Betty waited for an answer, so I just shrugged.

Meanwhile, Mom soaked some corn husks in a bowl of warm water.

"Have you picked a major yet?" Aunt Betty asked.

"Oceanography," I answered.

Mom looked up abruptly.

"Oceanography?" she echoed.

I braced myself.

"I never knew you liked oceanography," Mom said.

"What does an oceanographer do?" Aunt Betty asked.

"I'm planning on joining a research team," I answered.

"Researching what?" Mom prodded.

She looked dubious. It annoyed me.

I bit my bottom lip.

"Looks like you've given it a lot of thought," Mom snorted.

"Thanks for your support," I shot back.

"I am supportive," she answered defensively. "I'm just surprised by your sudden interest in oceanography. I always thought you'd end up in a more…"

She paused.

"I'd end up in a more what?" I demanded.

"A more…creative field," she shrugged.

"I have to finish my anthropology paper," I said.

I threw the final peels in the trash and headed to my bedroom.

"Homework again?" Mom frowned.

I stopped in my tracks and faced her.

"Yes, homework again," I said. "What's wrong with studying?"

Aunt Betty raised her right eyebrow. She mixed her bowl of *masa* with fervor.

"I just never see you anymore," Mom grumbled. "You're always in your bedroom."

"I bet if you saw me more, you'd complain that I didn't spend enough time on homework," I snapped.

Mom sucked in her breath sharply. I had embarrassed her in front of her sister.

I turned back toward my room.

"Charity," Aunt Betty pleaded. "Stay here. Help us make tamales."

"I'm not hungry," I told her.

By the time I reached my bedroom, they were whispering in urgent tones.

"Can't you wait until I'm completely out of earshot before you talk about me?" I shouted, as I slammed my bedroom door.

# The Cry Baby

I paced frantically around my room trying to grasp hold of my emotions. Tears sprung to my eyes, but I wouldn't let them fall, so I banged my fist against my desk. Pain reverberated through my hand. I felt instantly better.

Tears once flowed so freely from me. Mom even nicknamed me The Cry Baby when I was a little girl. I dissolved into tears at everything. If I scraped my knee, I wept like I'd lost a limb. Whenever someone snapped at me, I bawled. If kids teased me, I cried. Mom couldn't stand my tears.

"Don't be such a drama queen," she would scold.

Aunt Betty teased me about it constantly.

"You hold more water than a dam," she'd laugh.

Sometimes I didn't need a reason to cry. I'd lay in bed at night and tears streamed down my face - sometimes for an hour straight. I knew that most kids my age didn't cry or feel emotions as deeply as I did, but I figured I'd grow out of it. I was just going through some weird stage, right?

Now I wonder if it was a phase. Could I have had serious depression even as a child? Maybe I just didn't know it then. I only knew that I cried a lot, and when I did, it triggered negative reactions from others. People in my life frowned on it or teased me. Crying equaled bad, so I eventually learned to eliminate it with the help of cutting.

Mom sometimes remarked how moody you were, but maybe it took strength and guts to wear your feelings on your sleeve regardless of what anyone said or thought.

Perhaps if I hadn't let other people's reactions influence me, I wouldn't have such ugly scars on my arms.

# *Pain Relief*

I wasted my morning playing hearts, solitaire and black jack on my computer. Then I tried to read a book. As a kid I could easily escape into another world with a juicy piece of fiction. I couldn't focus, though. I read the same paragraph four times. I had zero concentration. Why did I feel so tired and burnt out all the time?

I flipped on the television. The same old episodes of the same old sitcoms, crime dramas and reality shows played. I clicked off the television and tossed the remote control on the floor.

My unmade bed beckoned me. I sighed heavily as I pulled my comforter over my head.

I later awoke to a dark room. I peered at my clock. I'd slept for nearly three hours. My head hurt, and my body ached. I couldn't find the energy to work on my research paper, so I turned on my TV and watched a documentary on blizzards until I fell asleep again.

I awoke two hours later to receive the silent treatment from Mom. When I walked into the kitchen for a drink, she stood alone at the sink scrubbing a big pot. You can tell Mom's angry when she washes dishes by hand instead of throwing stuff in the dishwasher.

I poured myself a glass of apple juice. Mom's lips were pursed and the vein in her forehead stuck out. She wouldn't look at me.

"I'm going back to my room to study," I announced, half-hoping she would object and we would resume our argument.

She ignored me.

Back in my room, I climbed into bed again. I wanted to regain the peace I found in sleep, but I felt too wired. I stared at the ceiling and tried unsuccessfully to will myself to sleep.

Suddenly, I heard the front door close. Mom had likely left for her weekly grocery shopping trip.

I rolled out of bed and roamed the apartment aimlessly. Seconds later I stood in our main bathroom. I opened the medicine cabinet and scanned the shelves.

Two prescription bottles sat on the top shelf. One held an antibiotic; the other contained painkillers. Our dentist prescribed the medication to Mom after she had a root canal last summer. I grabbed two painkillers and stuffed them into the pocket of my jeans.

I wandered into Mom's bedroom next. It looked spotless as usual. A picture of me in my high school cap and gown sat on the nightstand next to her neatly made bed. A tidy stack of crossword puzzle books lined a wicker basket on the floor.

"Why can't we talk about anything?" I asked the empty room.

I rummaged through her dresser drawers hoping to find a dark secret that would help me understand her better. I found nothing except perfectly folded clothes, potpourri and bottles of lotion.

When I returned to my bedroom, I washed down a painkiller with water and slid back in my bed. 20 minutes later a newfound indifference washed over me. I felt unusually calm and relaxed. Before long, I fell fast asleep.

# Monday morning – 2:15 am

Mom and I are on speaking terms again. Last night I walked into the kitchen and the aroma of homemade spaghetti filled the room.

"I'm making dinner," Mom said casually.

"It smells great," I answered.

I hovered awkwardly under the door frame.

"My hands are full," she said. "Can you grab me the colander?"

I walked to the cupboard. My hands shook as I reached for the stainless steel utensil. I took a deep breath and faced my mother.

"Mom," I said. "I just want to…"

"I'm making homemade bread, too," she added quickly.

I nodded.

I had experienced this drill many times already. Mom didn't want to discuss our argument. She never wants to contend with any clumsy words or emotions. Mom had implied that I should drop the subject, so I did.

# *Monday*

I'm writing to you from the mall food court. As I walked the shopping center earlier, I passed a closed storefront. Children's drawings of California's missions decorated the wall.

In fourth grade I wrote a report on the San Gabriel Mission. I labored at the library taking painstaking notes. Later, I printed my report and enclosed it in a clear blue folder. I decorated the cover with stickers that I had purchased from the mission's gift shop.

Then I turned my attention toward part two of my assignment: a diorama. I struggled with it. In the end my mission looked like a dumpy shack with a frightful paint job.

On the morning of the project's due date, I squirmed in our car's passenger seat trying to salvage my model.

"You put a lot of time into your project," Mom praised.

I didn't answer. I scrambled to fix a church bell that had fallen lopsided.

"I'm sure Ms. Lawrence doesn't expect a perfect looking diorama," she assured me.

By the time we reached Willard Elementary School's parking lot, I slumped resigned in my seat. The bell had fallen off completely when our car hit a speed bump.

Mom dropped me off with a kiss and a "good luck." Once her car disappeared from sight, I dropped my project into the nearest garbage can. I refused to turn in the flawed mission.

Ms. Lawrence gave me an A+ on my written report and an F on my missing artwork. I received a combined grade of C-.

At that point in my childhood, I harbored an obsessive need to strive for perfection in every area of life. I meticulously cleaned my bedroom every day. I completed chores without Mom's prodding. I even brushed my hair exactly 55 times a day.

School bore the brunt of my perfection. I strove for A's in all subjects. My ferocious commitment exhausted me. I didn't have time for fun activities; I had to study. I got buried in crafting perfection.

Taking notes became my new obsession. Every week I wrote all the knowledge I'd learned on a stack of note cards. I clung to my cards. I read them on the drive to school every day. I memorized them as I waited for Audra to pick me up from after-school daycare or when I brushed and flossed my teeth.

I even once brought my cards to the dinner table, but Mom put her foot down.

"You're getting carried away," she scolded. "Put those cards away now."

I also stored a flashlight under my mattress and studied after I'd gone to bed. Most nights I'd fall asleep with my note cards in one hand and my flashlight in the other.

I had my simple life under control. Except, little did I know that my quest for perfection would soon face a major roadblock.

# *Syllables*

In fifth grade history class, I breezed through an entire test with a cocky confidence. Then I reached the final question. Name three troubles the pioneers experienced on their way west. Halfway through my detailed explanation, disaster struck. I spelled pioneer with only one E.

When I used my pink eraser to correct my mistake, it left a telltale smudge on my paper. I tried to erase the ugly smear but the mark only grew bigger. Dismayed, I kept erasing the smudge. The weakened spot in the paper eventually ripped. I stared helplessly at my test.

When Mrs. Skinner instructed us to pass our tests forward, I slipped my sheet inside my desk and folded my hands in my lap. No way would I turn in my muddled paper, even if it meant flunking the exam.

The next day Mrs. Skinner asked to speak with me after class.

"What happened to your test, Charity?" she asked.

I stared at the tile floor in shame.

"I was so surprised when I graded papers last night and didn't see your test in my pile," she persisted. "I even checked my car to see if your exam had fallen under a seat."

I shifted my history book from one hand to the next and silently counted the floor tiles.

Mrs. Skinner waited for an answer. I didn't offer one. Finally, she spoke again.

"You're one of my best students, Charity," she said. "It saddens me to give you an F, especially when I haven't the foggiest idea why this happened."

I counted the paper clips in a cup on her desk.

"If you were having difficulty with the subject," Mrs. Skinner stressed, "I would have gladly helped you."

I didn't answer.

"You can always come to me if you need help, but you can't just refuse to take a test," she told me.

I wasn't stupid. I wanted to assure her that I would have gotten an A+ on the test if the dumb eraser incident hadn't happened. My cheeks burned as she recorded a 0 next to my name in her grade book.

I know what you're thinking. Why didn't I just swallow my pride and turn in the test anyway, smudge and all? I still would have scored an A.

By that point in my life, I found it crucial to achieve an A with absolute perfection in every aspect of the journey. If I couldn't complete a mission perfectly in every stage, I didn't want to finish it at all. I had a choice: take a flawed A or none at all.

When my report card arrived in the mail, I'd earned six A's and a B in history. I felt like a failure.

To top off my disappointment, Mrs. Skinner wrote a negative note under the comments' section:

> *"I think Charity believes she must be perfect all the time. It concerns me."*

Mom felt thrilled with my grades, though. She took me out for a burger and a movie to celebrate. I sulked the whole time. I couldn't stop thinking about the imperfect B that tainted my report card.

I mulled over Mrs. Skinner's comment. It confused me. How could wanting perfection be wrong? Weren't we instructed to always try our best? Why did Mrs. Skinner treat my outstanding efforts as a bad thing?

My mind wandered during the movie. I leaned back in my seat and stared listlessly at the lights in the ceiling.

"Are you feeling OK?" Mom whispered.

I nodded.

I tried to push the B out of my mind. I couldn't.

Finally, I occupied my mind by counting. I silently counted to 100. It relaxed me.

Before I could start thinking about that B again, I counted backwards from 100.

For the next two hours, the movie played but I wasn't part of its captive audience. I had created my own little world where counting reigned.

# The Meanest Thing I Ever Said

I haven't gone to school in over a week now. Mom still has no idea that I'm a college dropout.

I've gotten sloppy, though. Aunt Betty called a few minutes ago. I picked up the phone forgetting that I should be at school during the day.

"Hello," I said absentmindedly.

"Cherry?" Aunt Betty asked.

I couldn't pronounce my name correctly as a little girl. I called myself Cherry. The name still pops up sometimes, even though I asked Aunt Betty and Mom several years ago to just call me by my given name.

"Yep," I answered.

"What are you doing home?" she asked.

"I'm leaving for school in a bit," I lied.

"I expected to reach the answering machine," Aunt Betty said. "I'm returning your mom's call. She wanted my chicken pot pie recipe."

"Oh," I answered.

I made no effort to hide my lack of interest.

"Can you write down the recipe for your mom?" she asked.

"I'm leaving for school now," I lied again. "Can you call back in a minute and leave it on the voice mail?"

"No problem," Aunt Betty said.

I hung up.

I can't explain why Aunt Betty gets on my nerves. I feel guilty. You should like your relatives, right?

She's always nice to me - supportive, dependable, and loving. Yet, I feel unsettled around her.

Aunt Betty never married. In her early 20s she dated a man named Albert. He sold commercial real estate.

One day he flew to Texas to care for his sick sister. He promised Aunt Betty that he would be back in two weeks. He never returned to California.

When I was nine I told Mom that if I were Albert I wouldn't have come back for Aunt Betty either. She said it was the meanest thing I had ever said, and she hadn't raised her daughter to be so rude.

If she only knew all the awful things I've thought but have never said aloud.

# "Sick"

Mom came home for lunch today  I laid in bed watching some self-help show when I heard her voice in the hallway.

"Charity?" she asked.

She startled me. I nearly jumped out of bed, but I quickly composed myself and snuggled further into my blankets. I shut my eyes when she tapped lightly on my door.

"Charity?" she called out again.

I remained as still as possible. Finally, the door opened.  She stood at the archway watching me. After a few seconds she tiptoed to my bed and placed her hand on my forehead.  My eyes flickered at the unexpected contact, so I offered my best impression of a sick person emerging from a deep sleep.

"Are you not feeling well?" she frowned.

"What time is it?" I mumbled.

I faked looking dazed as I squinted at my clock.

"12:30," she answered. She reached for the remote control and lowered the TV's volume.

"Are you sick?" she repeated.

I nodded.

"What's wrong?" she asked.

"Headache," I lied. "Bad sore throat, too."

She touched my forehead again.

"You don't have a fever," she said. "Did you take anything for your headache?"

I shook my head.

Five minutes later she returned with a tray that held a chilled water bottle, two aspirin and cough drops.

"Sit up for a second," she ordered.

I sat up. Mom eyed my long sleeved shirt. She set down the tray, walked over to my dresser and tossed me a tank top.

"Put this on," she said. "You shouldn't be so bundled up."

I changed the subject.

"Can I have the aspirin?" I asked.

She handed me the water and two pills.

"Why are you home early?" I asked, as I swallowed the aspirin.

"I needed to change my new shoes. They were killing me," she answered, as she glanced around my room.

"I'm going back to sleep," I said.

I closed my eyes and turned toward the wall.

Mom stood staring at me. I felt tempted to ask her why she wouldn't leave.

Finally, she left. Five minutes later I heard the front door close.

I tried to drown the bad thoughts stewing in me. When that didn't work I walked into the living room and out on the patio. A plane flew overhead. I imagined all the passengers on it. I wondered where they were headed and who waited for them at the end of their destination.

When I walked back to my room, I noticed a note taped to the door.

*Charity,*

*I'll call you later to see how you're feeling. There are popsicles in the fridge. They might cool your sore throat.*

*Love, Mom*

I crawled into bed and reached under my mattress for a fresh razor.

# Tongue Tied

The summer before seventh grade I accelerated my counting obsession. I would walk into a room and count all the black objects, window panes, objects that began with a B, etc.

I also developed a specific bedtime routine. Every night I would open and shut my closet door 25 times. Then I would run my hand up and down my mattress 50 times. When I would finally settle down for the night, I'd circle my lips with my index finger 75 times. When I completed that, I would count to 200 and then backwards.

If I made a mistake, if I so much as stumbled, I restarted my entire routine.

By July I upped my rituals. I opened and shut my door 150 times. I ran my hands down my mattress 175 times. My index finger circled my lips 100 times. I counted to 500 and then backwards. Exhausted, I moved my bedtime up an hour to compensate for the lost sleep.

Life took a backseat to my new fixation. Counting devoured my time. I couldn't eat, drink, work on my homework or carry on conversations without the solace of counting.

I grew even quieter and more withdrawn. The outside world posed a threat to the inner sanctuary I'd created.

At school my classmates nicknamed me Tongue Tied.

"Hey there, Tongue Tied," they teased.

"Cat got your tongue, Tongue Tied?" they snickered.

Before long I tired of constantly seeing and hearing numbers, though. I needed a quicker solution, one that freed my schedule while letting me block out the chaotic outside world. I would soon discover cutting and embrace the quick fix it offered me.

# *Demotion*

My slide down the academic ladder officially commenced halfway through seventh grade.

At the start of the second semester, we took standardized tests in every subject. The school wanted to ensure that they placed their students in classes that matched their learning abilities. The slower kids in the more difficult classes were sent down a level, while the smarter kids in lower levels were promoted. I sat in the top tier math class: Pre-Algebra.

I felt especially anxious on test day. I hadn't slept much the previous night, having spent much of it counting.

With my anxiety running high, I nervously flipped through my math test. There were 50 questions. I counted to 100. Then I counted backwards from 100. After that I counted every classmate who wore blue. Then I counted the white outfits populating the room, and so on.

Before I knew it, only 10 minutes remained of class. I tried to work swiftly, but I had sabotaged too much time. I only reached question 18. I flunked the test. My days in the gifted program were numbered.

Sure enough, a few days later, Mrs. Murphy approached my desk during homework time.

"Charity," she said. "May I see you outside for a moment?"

Thirty-two pairs of eyes looked curiously over at me. I shrugged and followed her out the door.

Mrs. Murphy attempted to break the humiliating news delicately.

"As you know we used last week's tests to evaluate our students' progress in their classes," she began.

I looked down. I knew what words were coming. That didn't make it any less embarrassing to hear. Suddenly, an ant by my sneaker became the most fascinating creature I had ever seen.

"We think you'd be more comfortable in a lower level math class," she said almost apologetically.

Translation: you're dumb.

"You're demoting me," I responded dully.

"We'll keep a close eye on your progress in applied math," she answered. "If you excel at it, we'll promote you back to Pre-Algebra."

Suddenly, I felt tired and defeated. I didn't care anymore. She could have declared they were sending me back to sixth grade and I wouldn't have fought the decision.

"OK," I agreed.

All eyes watched me when I returned to my desk to collect my belongings. I might as well have had "dummy" stamped on my forehead.

Losers populated applied math: smart kids who didn't believe in homework, hardworking students who had the desire to do well in school but lacked the brains, and freaks, like me. I felt mortified when I entered my new classroom, but I didn't feel out of place.

Mom discovered my demotion six weeks later when my progress report arrived in the mail. My grades had plummeted in all my classes.

Mom gasped as she stood in my bedroom holding my report. I'd received three C's and three D's. She gawked at the paper, as if the grades might magically improve if she stared long enough.

"Your grades are a disgrace," she said.

I didn't answer. I had no defense. No words could possibly ease Mom's anger.

"Mad doesn't begin to describe my feelings, Charity," Mom said. "What on earth happened to your grades?"

I shrugged.

"You have nothing to say for yourself?" she asked incredulously.

"Oh, now you want me to talk about my feelings?" I laughed sarcastically.

Mom stared at me. Her mouth hung open in disbelief.

"I don't understand this, Charity," she said. "You're a bright girl."

"Evidently not," I answered.

I silently recited the U.S. presidents in the order in which they were elected.

"Don't act smart with me," she snapped.

"OK," I sighed. "I'll act dumb."

"You think your progress report is funny?" she asked. "Do you think school is some joke?"

I didn't answer.

"What happened to Pre-Algebra?" she continued. "I thought you were taking it this year?"

I shrugged again.

Mom waited for a better answer. I didn't give her one.

"How can you justify such an inexcusable progress report?" she screeched. "Do you have anything to say for yourself except a couple of shrugs and smart ass replies?"

Mom's composure had sailed out the room. I really enjoyed it.

"No TV until your grades improve," she yelled.

"OK," I shrugged.

"No phone privileges either," she added.

"Like I have any friends to call," I answered honestly.

Mom's face almost crumbled in pity, but she quickly snapped herself back into anger mode.

"I'm contacting your teachers tomorrow," she finally said. "I'll ask them to assign you extra credit work. You will be under strict watch from here forward. I better see some improvement quickly."

She slammed the door in a huff. I smiled.

I looked up at the ceiling and counted to 200.

Later that night I walked to the kitchen to fetch a tangerine. I stood peeling the skin off the fruit and throwing it in our trash can.

Suddenly, I heard Mom's muffled voice coming from her bedroom. I tiptoed to the door and pressed my ear against it.

"Why?" Mom sobbed. "Why?"

I walked back to my bedroom and stared at myself in the mirror. I felt horrified by what I saw. I had a smirk on my face—your smirk. I had caused Mom pain just as you had. I let her down. My eyes even had that zombie look Aunt Betty had once used to describe you. I glared at my reflection.

"Idiot," I called out.

Then I slapped my face hard.

## *"Freak"*

I began hitting myself whenever I felt my actions warranted it. If I disappointed myself... If I upset Mom or anyone else... I would slap my face or I'd punch my stomach. Sometimes I'd even bang my head against a wall. No one could punish me better than I could punish myself.

By eighth grade C's and D's littered my report cards. Mom eventually stopped arguing with me over my grades. She would just sadly shake her head and give me the silent treatment for a few days. Then she'd slowly resume talking to me.

Soon I relied on self-harm to help me cope with more than just anger and disappointment. I learned that hitting also worked to dull hurt, embarrassment or any other overwhelming emotions.

One day in science class, I sat alphabetizing my classmates by last name when I suddenly noticed the classroom looking at me. Our teacher, Mr. O'Hara, glared at me.

"Care to join us today, Ms. Graff?" he asked.

My cheeks burned. The class giggled.

"Please describe photosynthesis to the class," he commanded.

I hadn't opened my science book in ages. I stared blankly at him.

"We're waiting, Ms. Graff," he said.

I cleared my throat then uttered, "I didn't have time to read the assignment."

"Of course, you didn't," he agreed. "How could you possibly have time for anything with all the daydreaming you do?"

The classroom snickered again. A voice from the corner of the room whispered, "Freak!" More laughter followed.

Tears formed in my eyes. I bit my lower lip hard. They weren't going to see me cry. I wouldn't show them any weaknesses.

Mr. O'Hara returned to his lecture.

Someone threw a paper ball at me.

Later as I left class, James Edelman, the notorious school bully, locked eyes with me. I braced myself for his taunting. He followed me out the door and into the corridor making choking noises at me all the while. The more I ignored him, the louder his gagging grew. I distracted myself by mouthing state capitals. James quickened his pace until we walked side by side.

Then he leaned into my ear and shouted, "Freak!"

A few kids looked over at us. Some offered sympathetic looks; others laughed. With his successful mission accomplished, James moved onto his next victim.

Tears reappeared. Frustrated, I walked quickly to the restroom and locked myself inside a stall. I fought the urge to breakdown in sobs. I counted to 50 but the emotions stormed inside of me.

Without thinking, I dug furiously through my purse until I found a metal nail file. I robotically pulled up my blouse's left sleeve and began filing my arm as if it were as hard as a finger nail. Pieces of skin flaked off my arm, scratches emerged and then dots of blood appeared. My skin burned intensely. I cried out in anguish.

My emotional distress faded from sight, though. The tears subsided. The bad feelings melted away. I felt instantly better despite the physical pain. I had regained control of my emotions.

For several months I scratched myself with sharp objects to dull smothering feelings. Eventually, I turned to a razor for self-harm. My new instrument drew blood easier and quicker.

Only once, six months into my cutting stint, did I question my unusual actions. What if I accidentally cut too deep one day? I didn't want to die. I just wanted to stop the confusing carousel of emotions.

"I'm scared something is wrong with me," I told Mom one day.

"Wrong how?" she asked.

"I have bad thoughts sometimes," I told her. "I have overwhelming emotions that scare me."

"It's just your hormones," Mom said. "It's called being a teenager."

"Sometimes it's a struggle just to get through a day," I said. "Or I want to cry for no reason. I have always felt...different."

"There's nothing wrong with you, Charity," Mom said impatiently. "You sound like your father. You *want* something to be wrong with you."

Was it really my fault? Did I just want to feel this way?

"One of my coworkers has breast cancer," Mom continued. "Now there's someone with a real problem."

Hot tears flooded my eyes. I stared at the floor in shame.

"Would you rather be her?" she snapped.

"Of course not," I whispered.

"So stop feeling sorry for yourself," Mom scolded.

After that exchange I convinced myself that my depression and intrusive thoughts were merely figments of my imagination. Anytime, I felt overpowering emotions, I silenced them by cutting. I was wrong to feel sadness or confusion when others were truly suffering. Cutting provided both a solution and the perfect punishment for my inexcusable feelings.

# *Others*

At first I believed that no one cut but me. I thought I'd discovered some secret technique of dealing with my emotions that nobody else knew.

Then one night I lounged on the couch flipping TV channels. I paused on a news magazine show. A teenager sat emotionless while a reporter questioned her regarding scars on her arms. The girl explained that she cut herself whenever she felt overwhelmed in her day-to-day life.

I watched in fascination. Other people cut themselves, too? Who knew the practice was so common that it had reached the mainstream media?

"Crazy girl," Mom clucked. "She's getting all the attention she craves."

I thought about my own scars. If cutters truly hurt themselves for attention, why I hadn't I shown my cuts to anyone? Why had I spent so many years hiding my scars? Mom didn't understand the motive behind cutting, but I didn't feel like teaching her.

Later I went online to research cutting. I discovered that many people cut: girls, boys, mothers and even fathers.

Now I know that I'm not alone. A lot of people cut themselves. That doesn't make me feel any better, though.

# Out of Bounds

Mom knocked on my door. I sat up in bed, pulled my Cultural Anthropology textbook off my desk and placed it on my lap.

"Come in," I called.

Mom walked into my room. She sat on the edge of my bed.

For some crazy reason I felt too vulnerable to look at her.

I stared out my window. Some children were playing kickball in the middle of the street. One large boy argued with the other kids.

"The ball went out-of-bounds," he shouted.

Mom began the conversation tentatively.

"Hi," she said.

"Hey," I answered.

She followed my gaze out the window.

"Those kids will break a car window someday," she complained.

I nodded. Her gaze rested on me. She searched my face for answers.

"What are you studying?" she asked.

"Anthropology," I replied.

"How's school?" she persisted.

"Fine," I answered.

An aching silence followed.

I couldn't look at her. I fidgeted with my hair and cleared my throat.

"Are you getting a cold?" she asked.

Before I could answer, she picked my robe off the floor and handed it to me.

"You should start taking your jacket to school," she advised. "We're getting into the heart of flu season."

"OK," I mumbled.

"What would you like for dinner?" she asked.

I wanted to shout, "Go away!" I didn't.

"It doesn't matter," I said.

"How's ravioli?" she asked.

"Sounds good," I answered.

It didn't sound appetizing, though. No food sounded good to me. I hadn't felt hungry for weeks.

"I can make turkey meatloaf if you don't want ravioli," she offered.

The large kid started cussing at the other children. He grabbed his ball away from the shortest kid and announced that the game had ended. Some kids booed. Others protested.

"Is there anything else you'd like instead?" Mom asked. "I can make you anything."

Mom sensed things were bad for me, but she wouldn't dare ask me about it.

My head pounded. Those awful emotions threatened to emerge. I had to stop them.

"I said ravioli sounds good," I snapped.

"OK," Mom quietly replied.

I'd hurt her feelings. She deserved an apology.

Mom sat silently for several moments. She fingered the lace trim on my comforter. She peered out my window and watched the kids who sat dejectedly on the curb as they debated their next course of action.

I flipped a page in my book.

Mom pulled loose fray from my comforter. She cupped the thread in her hands and smothered it as she drew her hand into a tight fist.

"I'll get started on dinner now," she said.

I nodded.

She took one more look at me before she closed the door.

# *Maybe*

Mom,

I wish you would ask me to confide in you, but you're not like that. I would love to talk to you about my feelings, but that's not me.

I want to tell you how scared I am. I see my world falling apart, and I can't glue it back together. It's like I'm watching my life as an outsider.

I'm so lonely, but the thought of being around others terrifies me. It's all so confusing.

What's wrong with me? Is this how Dad felt before he left us? Am I losing my mind?

Mostly I want to apologize for letting you down. I'm not strong like you. Sometimes I think I'm too sensitive for this world. I can't deal with simple emotions like sadness, embarrassment or anger. I can't even handle happiness.

I hope someday I'll awake to discover a magic cure that'll guide me to my newfound courage. I'll make you proud. I'll be everything Dad couldn't be.

Maybe someday I'll tell you my secret fears, and you won't be afraid to hear them.

# Tug of War

I battled tears again yesterday evening. I almost succumbed to all the sloppy feelings wearing me down.

Finally, I couldn't stand the struggle anymore. I grabbed my razor and carved aggressively into my skin. Blood came too easily. My sheets, pajamas and pillow all bore the telltale signs of my secret. I bled so much that I panicked and almost called Mom.

I grabbed my robe and wrapped it tightly around my arm. The throbbing sounded like a drum corps in my ear. Eventually, the pounding and then the bleeding subsided.

I'm scared. I don't want to die, but I'm not sure I want to live either. I don't cut myself because I'm trying to kill myself. I started cutting because it stripped away my confusion and pain. It comforted me.

Except, cutting didn't help me yesterday. My emotional pain remained. It didn't soothe me. I actually felt worse after I cut. If cutting stops being effective, what will I turn to next?

# Short Sleeves

I'd like to wear short sleeves in warm weather. I'm tired of hiding my secret.

My sophomore year of high school I walked to the drug store to buy more razor blades. I glanced at tabloid covers as I waited in the checkout line.

Suddenly, I noticed a girl in front of me in line. She wore a halter top. Cuts ran up and down both arms. They were clearly the work of a razor or scissors.

I had never seen another cutter in person. Intrigued, I inched closer to her. I tried to make eye contact, but I also feared she would notice me.

Finally, she turned toward me. She looked at me gawking at her scars. She smiled, big and bold, like her cuts were boast worthy. She wore her scars like a badge.

Her actions fascinated me.

What if I allowed the world to see my scars? Would my cuts anger or disgust them? Would people call me crazy? Or worse, would they say nothing at all?

# Something in Common

I felt better today. This evening I stopped by the gas station across the street for a cup of coffee. Then I walked to the beach and sat on my favorite bench overlooking the ocean. The orange sky looked gorgeous against the calm of the deep beryl sea.

I pulled my digital camera from my purse and snapped pictures with unusual enthusiasm. Then I sipped my coffee and watched the sun set.

A few minutes later, a man wearing a business suit sat beside me. We exchanged pleasant looks. He nodded before he disappeared into his thoughts.

I wondered what inspired that man to visit the beach. He'd obviously come directly from work. Maybe he'd just lost his job and he couldn't face his wife yet. Perhaps he'd nailed a sales call, and he wanted to share a quiet, personal celebration with the ocean.

As I stood to leave, I debated wishing him a nice evening. I decided against it. Whatever had drawn him to the beach, he'd chosen to come by himself. I wouldn't intrude on his alone time.

When I got home that night, I printed my photos. I spread them on my bed like a fan and examined my work. They weren't bad for an amateur.

I placed the pictures in a manila envelope and slipped them into my purse, so they'd always remain with me. I wanted a constant reminder that it felt nice to be good at something.

# Kaylee

I met Kaylee on our first day of kindergarten when she tapped me on the shoulder and admired the violet ribbons holding up my ponytail. She approached me again during recess as I stood panic stricken by Mrs. Friedman.

"Come play on the jungle gyms with us," Kaylee gently ordered.

She grabbed my hand and pulled me toward some other girls who waited for her.

"We're playing house," she informed me.

I felt so grateful she sought me out that I didn't object when she asked me to switch shoes with her until the end of recess. I wore knock-off Mary Janes, and she despised her brown leather shoes with thick white soles. It felt so forbidden to trade shoes with someone. A tingle tickled the back of my head.

Kaylee and I quickly became best friends. I don't know why she chose me as her number one friend, but I felt honored.

Kaylee differed from other girls. She had a boisterous laugh that eclipsed any grown-up's. In fact, even adults seemed enamored with her.

She even refused to run when boys chased her. She'd stand with her arms on her hips daring them to come closer. They wouldn't.

The first few school years breezed by. Every day felt like one big party with the guest of honor. With Kaylee by my side, I never felt self-conscious or inadequate. Bullies stayed away from me. Girls didn't judge me. People left me alone.

No one paid attention to me, not when I had Kaylee as my best friend. People watched Kaylee, whether she sang the solo in the school Christmas pageant or she sat quietly reflecting. She never tried to grab anyone's attention, though. People were just naturally drawn to her.

Then in third grade, I lost Kaylee. The law firm where her dad worked announced a relocation to Seattle, Washington. Kaylee's father agreed to follow.

I comforted Kaylee when she broke the news to me. She looked so fragile in that moment. Her frail shoulders quaked under the strain of tears.

"What if I don't make any new friends?" she asked.

I almost laughed. She was Kaylee. How would she not make friends?

Thirty minutes later, Kaylee, resilient as always, rode her bike down the street. Her laughter bounced off the trees lining the neighborhood. Her fleeting insecurities had vanished.

"I hope my new bedroom has a bathroom," she said breathlessly.

I smiled and tried to ignore the knot in my stomach. How would I possibly cope without Kaylee? I felt so safe, comfortable and protected in her enormous shadow.

The next two months crawled as Kaylee's family orchestrated their move. I dreaded a long goodbye. I wanted to remove her from my life quickly as if I were ripping off a band-aid. Meanwhile, Kaylee rattled on about her new school, the two-day car drive to Washington and the warm clothes she had bought for Seattle's rainy weather.

On her final school day, Kaylee held center court telling girls about her new two-story home with a spiral staircase. A small crowd gathered around her. They soaked up her words. They stared intently trying to memorize every detail of Kaylee. A sad aura filled the air that day. Even our teacher, Mrs. Cook, seemed reluctant to bid Kaylee goodbye.

I didn't expect to see Kaylee on her final day in California. She had packing to finish. She was planning for a future that didn't include me.

So, I spent that Saturday morning on the recliner reading a mystery novel. My stomach ached with dread.

Suddenly, I heard the familiar sound of her family's minivan stop outside our apartment complex. Kaylee cheerfully bounced up my apartment building's stairs one final time.

When I opened the front door, she threw her arms around me and held me tight. Kaylee had never hugged me until that moment. I could barely choke out a goodbye before she turned away and ran back to her waiting family. I shut the door and walked quickly to my bedroom, careful to avoid Mom's concerned eyes peering at me from behind her book.

Kaylee later sent me a postcard from Northern California en route to Washington. She vowed to write me every week. I didn't believe her, but I appreciated the thought.

After Kaylee disappeared from my life, the little confidence I had went with her. That's why it unsettled me when I walked into my classroom on Monday and all the girls' eyes watched me closely.

At lunchtime several classmates followed me to my usual spot under the tree. A few kids offered me a taste of their dessert. Three girls even clamored to sit next to me on the swings.

The following day some girls showed up to school wearing ribbons in their hair, just like me. I knew what they were doing, and it unsettled me. They wanted me to take Kaylee's place. They had appointed me as their new leader.

Except, I didn't want to emerge from Kaylee's shadow. I didn't like people looking at me, let alone emulating me. I shrunk from the attention. I mumbled my way through conversations. I turned down sleep over requests from girls longing to be my new best friend.

Kaylee wrote me every week during her first two months in Washington. She even called a few times. On my tenth birthday she sent me a Party Girl Doll. I always wrote her back, halfheartedly. I knew some girl in Seattle would soon take my place, and she'd have a new best friend. Her letters eventually became sporadic. They stopped altogether right before seventh grade.

Two weeks after Kaylee's departure, a savior arrived in the form of Gwen Andrews, a petite beauty from Atlanta, Georgia. Mrs. Cook even sat the new girl in Kaylee's old seat. Gwen boasted porcelain skin and a tiny nose. Her white satin hair band framed a cascade of soft red curls. By week's end most of the girls in my class sported curls and hair bands. Some even developed Southern accents. Everyone went back to not noticing me. I felt so relieved.

I found companionship in the form of Donna McDonald, a soft-spoken girl, who lived with her aunt for reasons I never asked. We struggled to make conversation at first. Eventually, though, we reached the unspoken agreement to eat our lunches mostly in silence. We carried on our barren friendship until 6th grade, when she, like most kids in my class, enrolled at Franklin Junior High, and I wound up at Jefferson Junior High.

By the time high school arrived, I no longer cared about the social stigma of eating alone, so I ate by myself every day.

My social life did not exist. I attended only one football game. It was the day our school played our cross-town rival, Long Beach Polytech, for first place honors. I forgot my jacket and sat miserably cold for an excruciating two hours and 20 minutes.

During halftime, all heads in our section suddenly turned toward the stairway. Gwen and her fellow cheerleader friends from Long Beach Polytech, had sauntered over to our section. They marched toward Brian Esparza, our star player, who sat on the bleachers sidelined with a broken leg.

As Gwen passed by my row, her eyes flickered across my face. She smiled distractedly at me, as if she knew me but she couldn't place how. She never knew how close I'd come to being her.

I walked to Kaylee's old house yesterday. It looked remarkably the same except a blue tricycle now sat on the driveway. I pictured Kaylee and me riding our bikes up and down the street pretending our Schwinns were horses.

I looked at the elm tree that enveloped the front yard. I remembered how I watched with horror as Kaylee tumbled to the ground after she tried to copy a gymnast's move from the Olympics.

I walked to the tree. I ran my hands over its trunk, as if by touching it, I'd conjure up Kaylee's spirit.

I hadn't thought of Kaylee in years. Now I missed her terribly. She wouldn't have tolerated my cutting.

I thought back to the time I tried riding my bike on the curb like boys did. I teetered and tottered before I finally crashed to the ground in a big heap. I scraped my wrists. My knee had a red chunk of skin hanging from it. I whimpered for Mom.

Kaylee picked up my bike and held out her hand.

"Get up," she ordered.

Her cornflower blue eyes were kind but firm.

"Your mother isn't home anyway," she informed me. "You'll have to handle this on your own."

Kaylee always made everything seem so easy. I picked myself up and followed her inside her house. She put iodine on my knee and blew on it.

Twenty minutes later I had jumped back on my bike. I'd forgotten all about the accident as I laughed hysterically at some corny joke Kaylee had just told me.

"You'll have to handle this on your own."

Kaylee's words haunted me as I walked back home.

# *Wilson High*

I can summarize my high school career in one fragmented sentence. Wake up, school, eat, homework and bedtime.

Although my graduation happened less than two years ago, I've already forgotten the little details at Wilson High, such as my English Literature teacher's name or our senior class gift.

Nearly every weekday at lunchtime, I left the school cafeteria with macaroni and cheese, a stale bread stick and watery diet soda. On adventurous days I'd order the lemon chicken and chow mein option.

I kept a low profile in my classes. Teachers never expected me to contribute toward discussions. Of course, I never caused disruptions in the classroom either. I rarely spoke to my teachers and classmates, and they barely looked at me.

After school I'd hang out at the library reading a book until evening. Then I'd walk home and microwave whatever dinner Mom threw together that night. I'd usually eat in my bedroom while watching the 6 p.m. newscast full of ordinary folks in extraordinary circumstances.

After dinner I'd finish my homework, shower and head to bed around 11 p.m. Then I'd wake up the next morning and my robotic cycle would repeat itself.

My routine didn't change much when I started Long Beach City College. I continued my humdrum existence - until Professor Gaines entered my life.

# *Speechless*

I sleepwalked through year one of college, exalting in the carte blanche higher education offered. Except, responsibility must accompany freedom, and my negligent behavior obliterated my comfort zone.

It started out a normal day. I'd cut the previous night and nearly overslept for Cultural Anthropology. I quickly poured myself some apple juice before heading out the door.

I drove to school in my usual daze, so zoned out that I didn't even notice a dip in the road. The car bounced roughly just as I sipped from my cup. Juice spilled everywhere.

After I parked my car, I pulled a spare sweatshirt from my backpack. Then I walked toward my classroom's building.

I dropped my backpack on the floor of the empty restroom and stripped off my stained sweatshirt. I caught my reflection in a full-length mirror. My tank top showed off the unsightly cuts running up and down my arms. I inched closer to the mirror in morbid fascination.

I had fallen into such a trance that I didn't notice Professor Gaines had entered the restroom, until I turned around and came face to face with her. She stared at my arms, her eyes wide with horror.

Color drained from my face. I gaped at her. She gaped back at me.

I told myself to say something, anything, but words failed me. Old Tongue Tied had reared her ugly head again.

So, I threw my sweatshirt over my head, smiled at her like an idiot and hurried out the restroom.

## *Hunter*

I ditched class that day. What could I possibly say to Professor Gaines? What valid excuse could I offer for my scarred arms and subsequent odd behavior?

I planned to drop Cultural Anthropology from my class schedule. I'd take the course from a different teacher the following semester. I counted on Professor Gaines being a typical college professor who stayed out of her student's business. In a few days she'd forget all about the incident. Just to be safe, though, I confined myself to the north side of campus, so I wouldn't run into her.

Unfortunately, I had deluded myself. It took Professor Gaines only a week to find me.

Around 11 a.m. I sat soaking the sun near the science building. I munched on a glazed donut while reading a magazine's list of the world's sexiest men. Suddenly, a shadow loomed over me. I looked up. Professor Gaines stood before me.

"Hi," I said uncertainly.

"Hi, Charity," she answered.

*She actually knows my name.*

Professor Gaines held a coffee cup in one hand. My heart rate quickened. I forced a smile.

She cleared her throat.

"Have time for a quick conversation?" Professor Gaines asked.

*Oh no.*

She sat beside me.

I told myself to smile brightly, but my facial muscles would not comply.

"What's up?" I asked.

Professor Gaines rested her thumb on the rim of her mug. She fingered it thoughtfully, as if she were carefully deliberating each word she spoke.

"I haven't seen you in class lately," she began.

"I had a cold," I said. "I plan to be at the next class."

*Darn it. So much for dropping Cultural Anthropology.*

"That's good, she answered, "because I've been concerned about you."

I feigned surprise at her comment and cocked my head quizzically.

"Concerned?" I echoed.

A janitor nearby grappled with inserting a fresh trash bag into a large, smelly waste receptacle. I would have changed spots with him in an instant.

"I saw your arms the other day," Professor Gaines reminded me.

I didn't have an answer prepared.

"Is there anything you'd like to tell me?" she asked easily.

"I don't think so," I answered in a small voice.

"How are you handling your classes?" Professor Gaines asked.

"Great," I answered quickly.

"What about your home life?" she prodded. "How's that going?"

"Wonderful," I replied.

"Do you live at home?" she asked.

"Yes," I answered. "I live with my mom. We get along great."

"I'm glad to hear it," Professor Gaines answered.

A torturous silence followed.

"Why do you have cuts all over your arms?" she finally asked.

Her bluntness floored me. She watched my face carefully as I searched for an answer.

"I had a small accident before class," I answered slowly.

*Think of something. Anything.*

"My cat scratched me up pretty badly," I offered.

I turned red. My eyes shifted. I'd created the world's lamest lie. As far as convincing excuses went, I'd just earned a fat F.

"You must have a big cat," Professor Gaines joked.

I smiled weakly.

She sipped her coffee. Her gaze never left my face. I tried not to fidget.

"Well," she said, "I think it would be a good idea if you met with a friend of mine. His name's Hunter. He works in the counseling center. He's an excellent therapist."

I tried to appear calm.

"Why do you want me to talk to him?" I asked.

She ignored my question.

"He's a real easygoing guy and very popular with the kids," Professor Gaines said.

I didn't answer.

She flipped open her cell phone.

"I called him last week," she said. "He can see you on short notice."

My mouth went dry.

"Would you talk to him for me, Charity?" Professor Gaines asked.

How could I say no without sounding like the world's biggest jerk?

Before I could respond, she had dialed Hunter's number.

"He has worked here nearly two years now," she told me cheerfully. "His predecessor left to start a private practice and…"

I stopped listening. I sat defeated. I'd lost the battle. My careless actions had ruined everything. Why hadn't I pulled my sweatshirt off in a private stall? Why did I stop so long to examine my scars?

Now a trained therapist would grill me for a full hour. He might as well strap me to a lie detector.

Professor Gaines' voice cut through my thoughts.

"Charity?" she asked.

"Yes?" I answered dully.

"I asked if you had a free hour right now?" she repeated kindly. "Hunter can see you right away."

I weighed my options. Professor Gaines wouldn't let this matter drop easily. I might as well get it over with.

"Tell him I'll be right over," I answered.

# *Suckered Into Therapy*

On the walk to my appointment, I debated running to the parking lot. I could drive home early or crash in a movie theater for a few hours. Common sense prevailed, though. Hunter would just tell Professor Gaines that I missed my appointment. Then she'd find me again and…

"Maybe it won't be so bad," I told myself.

Ten minutes later I sat across from Hunter, a slight man, no older than 30. He had a friendly face and deliberate speech.

"Hi, Charity," he smiled. "How can I help you?"

Now why would he ask such a question? Hadn't Professor Gaines told him everything?

"I don't know," I shrugged.

"Professor Gaines expressed concern about you," he said casually.

"I guess," I answered.

Maybe Professor Gaines hadn't told Hunter why she wanted him to see me. I could possibly wiggle out of this situation easily.

"I didn't turn in my last paper," I offered. "Maybe my forgetfulness worried her. I'm OK, though. I'm just dealing with an early case of senioritis."

"Tell me more about your senioritis," he responded kindly.

"Oh, you know," I answered evenly. "I worry about graduation and my future career."

Hunter smiled, "What's your future career?"

"Uh, I have no idea," I laughed. "I guess that's why I'm worried."

Hunter laughed with me. I relaxed.

"Well, you're still young," he said. "You'll probably change your major a dozen times before you settle on a career choice. There's nothing wrong with taking your time to choose the right path."

I nodded.

"We offer some wonderful career counseling seminars," he continued. "You should attend one."

I played along and acted interested.

"I'd like that," I said.

"Don't worry," Hunter smiled. "You'll make it through college in one piece."

I returned his smile, making sure to maintain eye contact with him.

"Well, thanks for your time," I said cheerfully.

I reached to the floor to gather my backpack.

"One more question," he said. "Have you ever intentionally harmed yourself?"

Blindsided.

I froze. No one had ever asked me that question. I pretended to lose my grip on my bag.

I hoped my stall technique would offer me time to conjure up a suitable answer. It didn't. I placed my backpack on my lap. I stared at Hunter. He stared back.

"May I see your arms?" he asked.

# Too Late

That's how my therapy stint began.

Hunter wanted to see me once a week. I didn't argue. I attended our weekly appointments, but I had a lousy attitude.

Professor Gaines and Hunter had a problem with my cutting. I felt fine with it. Why should I stop cutting just because it bothered them?

Now, I regret my attitude. I wasted fifty minutes each week behaving like a sullen brat. I clung to my stubbornness when I should have acted like an active participant in my therapy. Hunter wanted to help me, and I'd blown him off.

Maybe I'd have already stopped cutting by now if I'd opened up to Hunter from the beginning. I likely wouldn't have dropped out of school and spent the last few weeks clinging to my bed. Maybe I would have become a productive person if I'd stayed in therapy.

I could never return to Hunter. I'd practically spit in his face. Why would he want to help me now?

# My Future Life

As a young girl I always thought I'd marry around age 25. I'd have a hard-working husband and a sweet little daughter. When I'd leave for work in the morning, I'd wave at my neighbors and they'd wave back.

I thought I'd carve an exciting career in medicine or acting. Every night at dinner my daughter would feed our Boston Terrier food scraps under the table, and I'd pretend not to notice.

More and more I realize that I won't ever have that life. I'd have to actually leave the apartment to meet someone. No guy will ever happen to walk into my bedroom. Even if he did, I'm not exactly the greatest conversationalist. What would we talk about? My life centers on naps and TV shows. How could I ever show my cuts to a guy I liked? He would run away from me instantly. I wouldn't blame him.

All my life I've set my sights on becoming anyone but you. I never wanted people to view me as wasted potential. Could-Have-Beens are even more pathetic than Has-Beens.

No one dreams of becoming a loser, a failure or a joke. Yet, I'm all of those things now. I'm you.

# Half of Me

Things turned ugly between Mom and me tonight. When I walked through the front door after a double feature at the two-dollar movie theater, Mom stood up from the couch. She looked steamed.

"Sit down, Charity," Mom ordered.

I sat across from her and braced myself.

"Where have you been every day?" she asked.

"What do you mean?" I responded. Though I knew exactly what she meant.

"A Professor Gaines left a voice mail message," Mom said. "Apparently, she hasn't seen you in class for weeks. She wanted to know if you were feeling all right."

I looked at the floor.

"Have you been skipping school?" she asked.

I counted the syllables in her last sentence.

"Don't do that," Mom snapped. "Don't zone out. Answer me."

I sighed.

"I quit school," I admitted.

Mom covered her mouth with her hand.

"What?" she asked. "Why are you throwing away your education?"

"I don't want to go to college anymore," I said. "Maybe I want to explore other opportunities."

"Then you come to me," Mom answered. "You talk to me. We discuss your options."

"Talk?" I asked. "Since when do we talk? We don't talk, at least not about anything substantial."

"So, it's my fault?" she fired back. "Are you blaming your dropping out of college on me?"

"Did I say that?" I asked, my voice growing louder.

"You don't say anything," Mom accused. "You don't talk anymore. You're a zombie. You walk through life in a daze. I can't stand to watch you anymore."

"So don't watch," I told her. "Keep pretending you don't know how messed up I am, just like you did with Dad."

Mom's bottom lip quivered, but she quickly composed herself.

"Don't turn this around on me," she barked. "I want a decent explanation for why you've dropped out of school."

I bit the inside of my mouth.

"Charity?" Mom prodded. "Answer me."

"I don't have an answer," I replied in an exasperated tone. "I don't know what to say anymore."

"You can start by telling me why you lied to me for the past few weeks," she responded bitterly.

"You don't want the truth," I said. "You don't want to hear anything messy."

"Why do you have all this hostility toward me?" Mom asked. "You made a mistake. You dropped out of school and didn't tell me. What gives you the right to act as if I did something wrong?"

I didn't respond.

"Answer me," Mom commanded.

I silently recited the alphabet backwards.

"Say something, damn it," she screamed.

I stared fascinated at her as she came unglued.

"Speak!" she yelled. "You look just like…"

She fell silent.

"Just like Dad," I finished.

She looked at me in surprise.

"You think I don't know?" I asked. "I see it. I know how much I'm like him. I've spent my entire life fighting so hard not to be him."

Mom's anger switched to confusion.

"Why?" she asked.

"Because you hate him," I answered.

"I don't hate your father, Charity," she said. "I've never hated him."

"OK, fine. I chose a strong word," I replied. "Maybe you don't hate him. It's just that his…"

I swallowed hard.

"His depression frustrated you," I continued. "You never understood him."

I paused.

"You don't understand me either," I said quietly. "For years I've stifled half of myself. I convinced myself that if you saw the real me, you wouldn't like me. So I've kept it all inside. For years I've only been half of me. I've only shown the person I thought you wanted to see."

Mom looked away. I started sobbing. I couldn't stop.

"You can't even look at me," I said. "You see him in me. Don't you think it terrifies me? I stay up at night wondering if I'm slowly losing my mind."

"You're hysterical," Mom said quietly. "We can't have a conversation when you're like this."

"I've been in a bad state for years now," I yelled. "You've noticed, but you've never directly asked me about it. You never want to hear the bad stuff. You just hope it'll go away, so you don't have to deal with ugly emotions."

"We're through with this discussion," Mom said firmly.

"No, we're not," I screamed. "I'm tired of pretending it's OK that we don't talk about our feelings. I'm sick of only talking about the good stuff in life while we ignore the bad. I'm tired of acting like Dad never existed. I'm through pretending that a big part of him isn't in me."

I reached into my purse and tossed my envelope of pictures on our coffee table. Mom stared at them in confusion.

"I like to take pictures, too." I said. "I bet you didn't know that."

Then I ran to my room.

# I Want

I wasn't surprised when Mom didn't follow me. She just walked calmly into her bedroom after my outburst and shut the door. She probably called Aunt Betty to tell her how horrible I am.

I switched on my computer, browsed to an Internet search engine and typed your name in the search box. Zero results. It didn't surprise me. I've searched for you often, but I've never found any trace of you.

Where are you? What are you doing right now? How can someone just disappear?

What if I found you? What would you say if I contacted you? Would you be happy to hear from me, or would you run away again?

I want to see you. I want to ask you where you've been for nearly 19 years.

I want you to apologize for deserting me. I want to hear that you're unable to sleep nights because you're so disgusted by your actions. I want you to hate yourself for casting aside one of the few good things that ever happened to you.

I hope you beg for my forgiveness someday. I want your decision to haunt you for the rest of your life. I hope you will never forgive yourself.

If you can't give me all of that, then I hope our paths never cross again.

# Numb

Mom left for work the next morning - business as usual. She wrote a note on our kitchen whiteboard:

> *Charity,*
>
> *I won't be home for dinner tonight. There's chicken in the fridge. Heat it in the oven at 375° for 25 minutes.*
>
> *P.S.*
>
> *There are cookies in the pantry.*

Unbelievable.

I poured myself a glass of water. Then I walked back to my room and crawled into bed. I tried to sleep away the bad thoughts, but I couldn't relax. I kept replaying the previous night's argument.

I finally threw the covers off of me and headed to the main bathroom where I picked up Mom's bottle of painkillers. I had really cut into her stash over the past couple of weeks. Only three pills remained of the 14 I began with. I popped one in my mouth and then washed it down with water. I paused and then I swallowed a second pill and stuffed the bottle in my pocket. Then I went back to bed.

# *Help*

I didn't see Mom that entire day. I had fallen asleep for the night by the time she arrived home from work.

The next evening she acted as if our argument had never happened.

She tapped on my bedroom door.

"I brought home a pizza," she called.

"I'm not hungry," I answered.

Mom hovered by my closed door for a few seconds. I tried to use telepathy so she'd ask me to talk to her. She walked away without saying another word.

Anger ripped through me. I yearned for her to acknowledge the rift between us. My frustration boiled. I considered confronting Mom about her infuriating behavior and decided against it. I felt too drained for a confrontation or further disappointment. So, I popped my last painkiller.

I peeled off my sweatshirt and stared in my mirror just as I did that day in the restroom when Professor Gaines caught me. My white tank top showed off my scars. They were big, hideous, menacing.

I sat on the floor for several minutes waiting for the painkiller to take effect. It wasn't working fast enough.

Suddenly, tears formed in my eyes. Except, I let them fall this time. My nose and cheeks turned moist. I cried so hard that I couldn't see through my rainfall of tears. Loud, ugly sobs filled the room. My shoulders shook. I began hyperventilating.

Suddenly, my bedroom door flung open. Mom stood under the door frame with a half-eaten pizza slice in her hand.

Looking utterly confused, she took in my swollen eyes and red nose. Then she caught sight of the cuts that decorated my arms.

"My God, Charity," she whispered. "What did you do?"

"I stole your painkillers," I confessed, as I continued to bawl out of control.

Mom stared at me in disbelief. Her eyes were glued to my arms.

"I'm too exhausted to cut anymore," I told her.

# Getting Started

Mom and I sat in Hunter's office. She had taken a personal day. We waited for him to finish a conversation with his secretary in the lobby. Mom made a nervous clicking sound with her throat. I reached under my sweater and fingered my band-aids.

"Don't mess with the bandages," she warned. "You'll remove them. You don't want anything getting infected."

Hunter walked into the room. He sat down and offered us his effortless smile.

"What brings you back, Charity?" he asked. "Not that I'm not glad to see you."

"I'm worried about her," Mom said. "She's had some problems lately. She..."

Her voice trailed off.

"My mom knows I cut," I said. "I'm here to get help."

"Let's get down to work then," Hunter replied seriously.

# Changing My Behavior

I have an appointment tomorrow with that psychiatrist named Doctor Peters. Hunter thinks my cutting and mood swings might be indicative of a depressive disorder. He wants a doctor to evaluate me right away, so we can begin the proper treatment.

I'm resuming my weekly sessions with Hunter. We're going to work on controlling my thoughts and directing my actions in a healthier manner.

Doctor Peters may recommend medication - like an anti-depressant. Mom raised her eyebrow at that suggestion. She wanted Hunter to treat me with therapy. He explained to us that therapy might not be enough for now. The three of us agreed to sit down and discuss our options after Doctor Peters offers his diagnosis and recommendation.

After we left Hunter's office, we stopped at Shore House Café for a bite to eat. As soon as we dropped our menus, Mom asked if I planned to return to school. She said one day I might regret leaving. I didn't promise her anything. I can't think about the future right now.

We ate the rest of our meal quietly. Not once did Mom ask me why I stopped going to classes. She never brought up my cutting either.

When we returned home, Mom complained of a pounding headache and disappeared into her bedroom for a nap. I walked to the kitchen and watered a fern that looked a little dry. Then I sat on the patio and thought about the past, present and future. I wondered if you'd ever sought help for your problems.

I'm worried about my evaluation. I'm scared of possibly taking medication. What if it turns me into an even bigger zombie?

I've never talked to a psychiatrist. What if Doctor Peters says I'm crazy? What if I'm a hopeless case?

# Evaluation

Earlier today I sat alone in front of Doctor Peters. Mom waited in the lobby. I needed to handle the evaluation on my own.

"What do you use to cut yourself?" he asked casually, as if it were the most mundane question in the world.

Startled, I answered, "Uh, usually a razor."

He scribbled on a paper.

"What else?" he prompted.

"Sometimes I scratch myself with my fingernails," I said meekly. "I've also used a nail file and scissors."

Doctor Peters nodded as he scrawled some more.

Suddenly, I blurted out, "If I wanted to kill myself I would, but I only cut to relieve stress or dull emotions."

My admission stunned me.

"Do you hurt yourself in any other way?" he asked.

"I've pinched myself and slapped my face sometimes," I admitted reluctantly.

"Have you ever burned yourself?" he asked.

I shook my head.

"Do you have patients who burn themselves?" I asked curiously.

Doctor Peters nodded.

"How long have you engaged in self-harm?" he asked.

"I started about six years ago," I answered.

"Describe your family life to me," he said.

"I still live at home with my mom," I told him.

"And your father?" he asked.

"I don't know my father," I replied in a flat tone. "He left me when I was a baby."

"I'm sorry to hear that," Doctor Peters said.

"Any history of mental illness in your family?" he asked.

I paused. Doctor Peters waited.

"My father suffered from depression," I admitted.

My sarcasm suddenly kicked into high gear.

"Are you going to tell me that I cut because my crazy Dad left me?" I asked.

Doctor Peters looked amused by my remark.

"Do you?" he asked.

# *Together*

Mom and I ate lunch at Taco Beach. We discussed the menu as we waited for our food. Mom played with her straw wrapper by lightly wrapping it around her finger. I do the same thing when I'm nervous.

"How was your appointment?" she finally asked.

"OK, I guess," I answered.

"You were in there a long time," she commented.

"Doctor Peters believes I suffer from major depressive disorder," I told her.

Mom considered my words for a few minutes. Finally, she nodded.

"OK," she said, as if giving me permission to be depressed. "That's fine."

"Our food's taking a long time to arrive," Mom added, as she dipped a tortilla chip into a bowl of salsa.

"He thinks I use my cutting as a coping mechanism," I said.

"Oh," Mom replied quietly.

"I have trouble dealing with feelings, so I create physical pain to distract myself from my emotions," I explained.

Mom folded then refolded her napkin.

"How does one cure it?" she asked.

"You don't cure it," I told her. "You treat it. I have to learn to talk about my feelings instead of keeping them buried inside of me."

"I see," Mom replied quietly.

"He also prescribed medication," I said. "I can drop it off at the pharmacy anytime."

"Are you sure you need the medicine?" she asked dubiously.

"Doctor Peters said I've suffered a long time," I replied. "He thinks that an anti-depressant will level out my moods."

Mom nodded.

"The medication may also decrease my desire to cut," I explained. "Although, I need to continue discussing my feelings through therapy."

She didn't answer.

"I also count when I feel overwhelmed," I added. "That's why I look like a zombie sometimes."

Mom flinched and looked toward the kitchen.

"I see," she said softly.

I felt bad for Mom. I knew she found it difficult to discuss such unpleasantness.

Our waitress finally arrived with our food. I picked at my bean burrito.

"Mom, I have a confession to make," I said.

"Yes?" she answered.

"I'm scared," I told her.

"I am, too," she admitted hesitantly. "But we'll get through this together."

I searched my mother's eyes. She met my gaze with a protective determination.

Suddenly, I felt starved.

# *Words*

"How do you feel right before you cut?" Hunter asked.

I fell silent and stared out his office window.

"It's really hard talking about my feelings," I admitted.

"Of course, it's difficult for you," Hunter answered. "You've denied your emotions for so long."

I fidgeted with my hair.

"It will get easier," he assured me.

"So, how do you feel before you cut?" he asked again.

"It depends," I answered. "Sometimes I feel angry. Other times I'm sad or frustrated."

"And how do you feel about those feelings?" he asked.

"Smothered," I answered. "It feels like someone has placed a blanket over my mouth, and I can't breathe. It's as if I'm backed into a corner, and I can't get away."

"Go on," Hunter encouraged.

"Those suffocating feelings build until I can't fight them anymore," I continued. "Then I cut."

"How do you feel after you cut?" he asked.

I took a moment to consider his question.

"At first it hurts," I explained. "I can't feel anything but incredible pain. I can't think. I can't breathe. I only feel pain."

"And then?" Hunter asked.

"Once the pain stops, I feel immediate relief," I replied. "It's like someone has lifted an enormous weight from my shoulders."

"Go on," he urged.

"All those overwhelming emotions drain out of my body," I said. "All the bad thoughts disappear, and I feel at peace."

My voice cracked slightly. Hunter handed me a tissue. I wiped my nose.

"Do you want to know something?" Hunter asked. "You can find peace without cutting."

I paused, confused.

"How?" I asked.

"Through words, Charity," Hunter smiled kindly. "Through words."

# *"I Cut"*

This morning I sat on the living room floor organizing my new photo album when Aunt Betty barged through the front door and nearly stepped on me.

"Whoops! You almost gave me a heart attack," she exclaimed. "I didn't know you were home."

"What are you doing here?" I asked.

"I came to pick up my crock pot," she told me. "Your mother borrowed it last week. She said I could stop by today."

I nodded and returned to my pictures. Aunt Betty kneeled beside me and gazed at my photos.

"I never knew you had an interest in photography," she remarked.

"It's a fairly new hobby," I answered.

"Your father took some beautiful pictures," Aunt Betty said. "It looks like you inherited his talent."

"I've never seen his work," I said. "What kind of pictures did he take?"

"Everything. People, animals, architecture," Aunt Betty remembered. "He took gorgeous shots of the ocean. They were published in a calendar once."

"I never knew that," I exclaimed. "Why didn't you ever tell me?"

"I don't know," Aunt Betty shrugged. "I probably should have."

"He took some great photos of you, too," she added.

"He did?" I asked. "I've never seen them. Where are they?"

"You'd have to ask your mother," Aunt Betty told me.

I contemplated my next question. I knew what I wanted to ask, but I wasn't sure I wanted to hear the answer. Finally, I took a deep breath and plunged forward.

"Why did he leave?" I asked.

My question startled her.

"I'm sure you and your mom have had this conversation a million times," she said tentatively.

"No, we haven't," I answered. "Not once."

Aunt Betty fell silent.

"Of course, you haven't," she said almost to herself.

Aunt Betty searched the ceiling for answers. Finally, she spoke.

"Your father adored you," she told me. "He just had so many inner demons. He tried to get a grasp on them, but they eventually overwhelmed him to the point where he probably thought you'd be better off without him."

"Oh," I said.

Aunt Betty patted my knee.

"It wasn't anything you did," she stressed. "You were a sunny presence in his dark world."

"Did Mom love him?" I asked.

Aunt Betty mulled my question.

"I don't know," she finally admitted.

I nodded.

"She cared about him a lot," she assured me. "It's just that towards the end of their relationship, she suffered greatly."

"How so?" I prodded.

"She was so young herself," Aunt Betty explained. "Suddenly, she had to contend with a career, a baby and your father's issues. She hadn't counted on having to care for your dad, too."

"I see," I said solemnly.

"When she saw your father suffering so much, it frustrated her that she couldn't help him," Aunt Betty explained. "She took his depression personally, as if she was somehow at fault for not helping him more."

"That's ridiculous," I said. "His depression was not her fault."

"I know," Aunt Betty replied. "I know."

We stared at my photos again for a moment.

"I suffer from depression like he did," I blurted out.

Aunt Betty did not look very surprised by my admission. She nodded thoughtfully.

"I'm sorry, Cherry," she said sadly.

"Did Mom tell you I'm seeing a therapist and a psychiatrist?" I asked.

"No," she answered softly.

"I haven't been very productive lately," I admitted. "I have days when I can't even get out of bed."

"I had no idea," she said.

"I dropped out of school," I continued. "Did you know that?"

Aunt Betty shook her head in astonishment.

"Did Mom tell you that I cut?" I asked.

She wrinkled her brow.

"You what?" Aunt Betty asked.

I rolled up my shirt sleeve and showed her my scars.

Aunt Betty stared at my arm. Then she looked me in the eye.

"I had no idea," she said. "I've heard about people who cut themselves, but I didn't know you were one of them."

"I cut myself because I have trouble dealing with my emotions," I explained.

Aunt Betty nodded casually like we were talking about the weather.

"That makes sense," she replied.

"That's why I'm working with a therapist and a psychiatrist," I told her. "We're all working together to help me learn how to deal with my emotions in a healthier manner."

Aunt Betty nodded again.

"I'm proud of you," she said.

I looked down embarrassed.

"Do you realize this is the longest conversation we've had in a long time?" she asked.

I nodded.

"I can't believe Mom never told you any of this stuff," I said. "I thought she told you everything."

"No," Aunt Betty answered. "Your mom doesn't tell me much."

Her words surprised me.

"What do you two talk about then?" I asked.

"The weather, cooking, work," Aunt Betty said, waving her hand. "Superficial things."

"But if Mom doesn't talk to you about her personal problems, who does she talk to?" I asked.

"No one," she answered quietly.

I suddenly felt incredibly sad for Mom.

"Who do you talk to about your problems?" I asked.

"I don't have many close friends," Aunt Betty admitted. "I don't keep it inside of me, though. I write my feelings in a journal."

"I do, too," I exclaimed. "It makes me feel better."

"Me, too," she replied.

"Aunt Betty?" I asked.

"Yes, Hun?" Aunt Betty responded.

"If you ever need to talk to someone, you can call me anytime," I told her.

"That would be nice," she smiled. "The same goes for you."

After Aunt Betty went home, I realized why she made me nervous all those years. Her candor unnerved me. I wasn't used to it.

# *Someone*

I walked to the beach today. I packed a sandwich and some grapes. Then I sat on a creaky log on the sand and studied my surroundings.

Slowly, I unbuttoned my white button-down sweater and slipped it off, revealing a red tank top. My arms hadn't enjoyed the sun's inviting rays in years. I basked in the warm weather - bandages, scars and all.

A group of college guys howled as they played with a remote control airplane. A toddler gripped his mother's hand and walked cautiously into the ocean's current and then froze and squealed with delight as the water engulfed his feet. A young teen couple shyly held hands as they stood at the shoreline and gazed at the never-ending sea. I took photos of them all.

As I held my camera in my hands, I noticed one of the college kids staring at me. He waved. I looked behind me to ensure he'd directed his gesture at me. Then I waved cautiously back at him. He broke from his group and jogged toward me.

"Hey," he said breathlessly once he reached me.

"Hi," I answered tentatively.

"Where have you been?" he asked.

I looked questioningly at him.

"I haven't seen you in Art Appreciation in ages," he told me.

I studied his face. Then it hit me. I was talking to Brent What's-His-Name.

I ran through a list of excuses. Finally, I decided on the truth.

"I've been dealing with personal issues," I told him.

"Well that stinks," he said easily. "Are you ever coming back to class?"

"I doubt it," I said. "I've missed too much time."

"That's a shame," he said. "You're not dropping out of school entirely though, right?"

"No," I answered. "I'll be back."

My response surprised me.

"Good," he replied.

We didn't say anything for a few seconds.

"Well, I'll see you around, Charity," he finally said.

"Take care, Brent," I told him.

On my walk home, I replayed our exchange.

Someone had noticed me.

## My Own Conclusions

Mom made chicken cacciatore for dinner tonight. She sat in the living room munching on her meal and watching TV while I buttered my slice of French bread in the kitchen. Then I picked up my plate and headed toward my room. Halfway down the hall, I stopped in my tracks. Then I turned around and walked over to Mom.

She looked up immediately.

"You don't like the meal?" she asked.

"I'm sure it's very good," I told her. "I just thought I'd join you for dinner."

Mom made room for me on the sofa as I set down a coaster for my water.

"There's a high speed chase on the 405 freeway," she began. "A man came out of a..."

"Do you have Dad's pictures of me?" I cut her off.

"What?" she asked.

"Aunt Betty said he took some great photos of me," I said. "I'd like to see them."

She nodded thoughtfully.

"I think I can fish them out of my bedroom closet," she answered.

"I want to talk about Dad," I told her. "I'm through pretending that he's not an important part of me."

"Charity, I'm sorry if I ever gave you the impression that I disliked your father," Mom said sincerely. "I cared for him very much."

"I didn't know that," I answered. "How could I have known how you felt about him? You rarely talk about him, and the few times you have, your voice drips with contempt."

"I had much anger toward him when he left," she explained.

Mom paused for a moment, as if she debated saying her next words.

"I couldn't fathom how he could leave you," she said delicately. "So I kept my comments about him to a minimum, so I wouldn't disparage your father to you."

"So, I had to draw my own conclusions about him," I said. "That was difficult."

"I'm sorry," she replied softly.

She paused.

"You were right when you said I didn't understand him," she added. "His behavior really baffled me."

"Dad was ill," I told her.

"Yes," Mom agreed sadly. "I should have tried to help him more."

"There's only so much you could have done," I said. "He needed to want your help."

"You're probably right," she answered.

We ate quietly for several minutes. A fear gnawed away at me. I tried to shove it from my mind. Finally, I spoke.

"I'm scared I'll end up like him," I confessed.

Mom grabbed my hand and clasped it tightly.

"He didn't seek help for his problems," she said. "You are."

Her words comforted me. She returned to her dinner. I bit into my cacciatore.

"The chicken tastes delicious," I told her.

"Well," Mom said lightly. "I try."

We finished our meal in comfortable silence.

# My Life Now

Five weeks have passed. I begin my spring semester of college tomorrow. I'm taking Introduction to Photography. If I enjoy the class, I may take another one. Then again, I might find I'm good at something else.

Mom gave me a collection of your photographs. I'm making a collage. I'm in awe of your talent. I hope that someday I'll be half as good a photographer as you.

I cut the other day. Mom had a horrible day at work. She snapped at me for forgetting to unload the dishwasher. I called her a grouch in retaliation. Things got heated. I stormed off to my room and cut my left arm.

I'm probably going to cut again, too. It'll take time to relearn my coping mechanisms. I can't fix my problems overnight. Until then I just have to try my best.

Mom came into my room later that night and apologized for taking her bad day out on me. I told her I was sorry that I raised my voice to her. We bandaged up my cuts together.

Last Thursday, after many weeks of deliberation, I filled my prescription for an anti-depressant. I'm still debating taking the medication, but Doctor Peters assured me that I can stop taking it if I don't like the way it makes me feel. He said, though, that it may help even out my moods, which sounds good to me.

Each week I discuss my feelings with Hunter. I realize now that life's a work in progress. There are no neat, tidy endings.

There will be times when I mess up, badly. I have to accept that. No one is perfect.

I'm not writing to you anymore. I'm through wondering what I did to make you leave. What could a nine-month-old possibly do to drive her father away? Nothing. You left because you had many problems, but I wasn't one of them.

I have to apologize to you, though. You were never weak for being depressed. By the same token, I never wanted something to be wrong with me either. Depression is an illness just like any other illness. If you don't treat it, then you'll never get better.

I hope wherever you are, you're happy. I wish you peace of mind. I even hope that someday you'll have the chance to read these words.

I have to go now. Mom, Aunt Betty and I are driving to Los Feliz this afternoon. We're going on our first nature hike.

Goodbye, Dad.

P. S.

Yesterday as I walked to Ripley's Electronics to pick up a new memory card for my digital camera, I thought about this journal. I wondered what your reaction might be if you ever received it in the mail. I pictured your eyes growing wide in disbelief as you held the world's thickest letter. I paused for a moment to let the image really sink in. Then I laughed out loud.

*Coming Soon*
*Kaylee Shares Her Story*
*in*

# Kaylee: The "What If?" Game
### The Second Book in the SoCal Series

*"I play the 'what if' game all the time.*
*It's a really vicious game."*

"Do you remember Leo Nardelli?" I asked suddenly.

Mom closed one eye and searched her memory bank.

"Leo, Leo, Leo" she repeated. "Why do I remember that name?"

"Charity and I were massively in love with him," I reminded her. "We planned to marry him."

"That's right," Mom laughed. "You were both going to marry him in a beachside wedding. You would get custody of him on Mondays, Tuesdays, and Wednesdays, and Charity would have him on Thursdays, Fridays and Saturdays..."

"...and we agreed to share him on Sundays," I finished.

We howled at the memory.

"He had the longest eyelashes of any boy I have ever seen." Mom remembered.

"Yeah," I said dreamily. "He's a professional baseball player now."

"No kidding?" Mom said. "Good for him."

"You're destined for great things, too," Mom added. "I'm not just saying that because you're my daughter. You've always had that unique glow about you. Everyone has always told me how special you are. You're the kind of girl that people meet and don't ever forget."

"So what am I doing in a psych ward?" I asked.

# About The Author

Christine Dzidrums resides in Southern California with her husband and two sons. Her first novel, *Cutters Don't Cry*, won the prestigious **Moonbeam Children's Book Award** for the Young Adult Fiction - Mature Issues category. She previously coauthored the biography, *Joannie Rochette: Canadian Ice Princess*. Christine also recently completed the young adults novel, *Kaylee: The "What If?" Game*, the follow-up to *Cutters Don't Cry*. She is currently working on her fourth book entitled, *Life Before Elmo*, and the children's picture book, *Princess Dessabelle Makes a Friend*.

**www.ChristineDzidrums.com**

90059182R00075

Made in the USA
San Bernardino, CA
05 October 2018